The Mask of the Beggar
WILSON HARRIS

First published in 2003
by Faber and Faber Limited
3 Queen Square London WC1N 3AU

Phototypeset by Intype London Ltd
Printed in England by Mackays of Chatham Ltd

All rights reserved
© Wilson Harris, 2003

The right of Wilson Harris to be identified as author
of this work has been asserted in accordance with
Section 77 of the Copyright, Designs and Patents Act 1988

A CIP record for this book
is available from the British Library

ISBN 0-571-21774-5

2 4 6 8 10 9 7 5 3 1

by the same author

PALACE OF THE PEACOCK
THE FAR JOURNEY OF OUDIN
THE WHOLE ARMOUR
THE SECRET LADDER
HEARTLAND
THE EYE OF THE SCARECROW
THE WAITING ROOM
TUMATUMARI
ASCENT TO OMAI
THE SLEEPERS OF RORAIMA
THE AGE OF THE RAINMAKERS
BLACK MARSDEN
COMPANIONS OF THE DAY AND NIGHT
GENESIS OF THE CLOWNS
DA SILVA DA SILVA'S CULTIVATED WILDERNESS
THE TREE OF THE SUN
ANGEL AT THE GATE
CARNIVAL
THE INFINITE REHEARSAL
THE FOUR BANKS OF THE RIVER OF SPACE
RESURRRECTION AT SORROW HILL
JONESTOWN
THE DARK JESTER

THE MASK OF THE BEGGAR

Wilson Harris was born in New Amsterdam, British Guyana in 1921 and came to live in London in 1959. Since then he has been Writer in Residence at the Universities of the West Indies, Toronto and Queensland (Australia), Commonwealth Fellow at the University of Leeds, Visiting Lecturer at the State University of New York at Buffalo and at Yale, Visiting Professor at the University of Texas at Austin and Guggenheim Fellow for 1973. He has received honorary doctorates from the Universities of the West Indies, Kent at Canterbury, Essex, Macerata (Italy) and Liège (Belgium). His many novels include *Jonestown*, *The Guyana Quartet* and *The Carnival Trilogy*.

For
MARGARET
as always

NOTE

In *The Mask of the Beggar* a nameless artist seeks mutualities between cultures. He seeks cross-cultural realities that would reverse a dominant code exercised now, or to be exercised in the future, by an individual state whose values are apparently universal. He senses great dangers for humanity in this determined and one-sided notion of universality. He senses unconscious pressures within neglected areas of the Imagination that may erupt into violence. The roots of consciousness are his pursuit in a quantum cross-cultural art that brings challenges and unexpected, far-reaching, subtly fruitful consequences.

The West has implicit governance of the world in politics, economics, social and cultural values. This is a well-known fact. It may have started with the Conquest of the pre-Columbian civilizations of the Americas in the sixteenth century and the decline of the ancient civilizations of China and India.

The Mask of the Beggar is based on the disguise Odysseus adopts on returning to his kingdom in Ithaca. It is changed, however, into a holed or fissured face in which Chinese, Indian, African and European immigrants may be invoked in Harbourtown, an imaginary gateway into South and Central America. Quetzalcoatl, an ancient god of the Americas, comes into focus in an unusual way that adds mutual and implicit distinctions between figures that appear.

Well-nigh forgotten, ancient pre-Columbian imageries are explored. They offer new perspectives. European codes begin, it seems, to suffer a measure of transfiguration as they face faculties and creativities beyond their formal traditions. The language implied by the artist – in his sculptures and paintings and writings – is of quantum variation. It is necessary to remember that 'quantum' has a counter-intuitive meaning and this bears on the mystery of consciousness and gives to characters an independence not sustained by conventional art.

This independence is of extreme importance. It implies not an absolute position but the necessity of cross-culturality. It implies that no individual is paramount but needs to undergo changes in sharing in the making of a community that is ceaselessly partial in creative and re-creative membership as it struggles to understand itself in range and depth. Paramountcy has led to deadly dictatorships and to an incessant feud, however hidden, between man and man in which one state or party seeks a control over the others.

Intuition continues to help but needs to surrender partially at times to unexpected variations that are deeply concerned with a cross-cultural creation – in which Spirit through manifestations and pigmentations that are never absolute, mirrors consciousness in range and depth.

The artist is dumbfounded when he meets someone in the Street, who appears to be a Carnival dancer, and who is an exact, living copy of a sculpture in his studio that he calls the Mother of Space. This is crucial and leads to the arrival of other living copies of sculptures he has created, or has hidden, in his studio. Some have sprung from figurines or miniatures that he keeps hidden in his notebooks, out of guilt perhaps, and this is part of his Dream in meeting real people: that they have come to life from neglected resources in the closed Imaginations of the world that hide them in the archives of history.

The boundaries of certain Western artists are extended

beyond their centrality. Van Gogh, Oscar Wilde, Goethe are instances of these.

This is a very brief outline of a formidable theme, which carries in its variations historical figures such as Cortez (a master of the globe), Montezuma (the last independent emperor of Mexico) and Trotsky (who was murdered in Mexico by an agent of Stalin and who was intent on a 'permanent revolution').

All sculptures and paintings are partial and therefore capable of some measure of fulfilment in unexpected ways through cross-culturalities in Space and Time. The artist is of the view that he carries an inner sculpture in himself which provides him with an endless Stone of Time that he needs to explore and which makes wood, glass, paint, marble, and other substances into unconscious emblems of humanity. A mutuality between the unconscious and the conscious, in new variant ways, may offer a genuine, open unity woven from complex diversities.

A further word about 'quantum language'. A writer may write intuitively in a novel. Intuition may prove itself, may bring into consequence what a writer previously senses or knows so deeply it passes beyond his immediate sphere. A change occurs through profound and unusual intuition in the space-time of imaginative fiction and this alters the linearities of fixture and invention. The writer seems to move *psychically* across ages. The 'quantum' hand or arm extends this movement by bringing *unpredictable, counter-intuitive* resources into play. In the heart of this quantum, unpredictable sphere the figures the writer creates may turn on him (or her) and may create his imagination afresh.

The artist or author does not have absolute control of his creations but is subject to being created afresh by the characters (or character-masks) he creates. In this way there is no final creation since finality is ceaselessly partial and is subject to profoundest alterations.

The artist experiences an excitement, troubling and ecstatic, as he finds himself launched on pathways he never expected to travel and on which his intuition is aroused afresh.

There is a racial prejudice in traditions of Culture. This can be met with ideological protest but it persists and remains intact. Perhaps it may be eroded, if not entirely erased, by a new kind of imaginary fiction in which art questions itself on the instinctive natures of the ancient and the modern.

Anachar Cloots (French National Assembly)

Sergei Eisenstein (*Battleship Potemkin*) emphasized the collision of disparate and conflicting elements in montage in order to produce, in the synthesis, new concepts and emotions. He coined such phrases as 'overtonal montage' to refer to modulations on such levels as lighting and color, and 'intellectual montage' to describe collisions produced by the juxtaposition of objects with rich cultural implications (thus, he . . . seeks to discredit Orthodoxy by juxtaposing its religious icons and idols with Asian and African statues, which for his European audience would connote the primitive and superstitious).

Herbert Eagle, Non-Indifferent Nature

> Today he came as the beggarman of unreason.
> He has come in many disguises.
> In the darkness, in the light he comes,
> Telling me, advising me, lecturing me,
> Yet always assuring me of his humility.
> I sometimes wonder, can his humility
> Perhaps be the the greatest disguise of them all?
> And why to me? Am I more in need of him?
> Of his recollections, reflections, memories?
> He holds out his hand for alms
> Even as he tells me they are hands of healing.
> Oh beggarman of the world, and that other world,
> Servant and Master, beggar of two faces,
> Beggar of many faces,
> Clasp my hand and look into my eyes
> And teach me to understand.
>
> *Margaret Rose Harris, 'The Beggarman'*

Comings and goings not gotten over.
Death not gotten over, goings away
glimpsed again had us gone without
going . . .
  Nathaniel Mackey, 'Sound and Sentience'

To Go Under a Painting
Wave of wheat beneath a swarm of crows.
Which sky's blue? The one above? Below?
  Paul Celan, translated by Michael Mitchell

1

I have never forgotten the day my son came home with indescribable emotion and colour on his face and in his eyes. He refused to eat... It was noon. Time for lunch. Rice and vegetables. He stared at his plate. 'His face is there,' he said to me. 'The face of the Beggar at the corner of West Street.'

A strange sickness, unlike all forms of sickness I knew, and a darkness stood on him now. Was it terror? Was it loathing? Was it more than these, was it less, was it the inexplicable origins of art?

I felt with an illogical sensation perhaps that my son was destined to be an artist in the way he looked at me, at my troubled face, as if it were a picture he was making. What is art that makes one feel, all at once, like a Child? Had I become a Child in my helplessness? I was as troubled as he. I reached out and urged him to eat but to no avail.

A Child sees reflections of his mother in *living* glass, *living* wood, on which the sun strikes through the window to combine with emotions that become so vivid they are full of subtleties of darkness.

My son was eight years old but suddenly he seemed to me quite ageless, the oddest feeling to have. I tried to shake it off but it persisted in a far-flung corner of my mind. *Indeed it persisted as if it arose from him rather than from me. I was but a reflection*... Yet I knew, however wanderingly, as reflections always do, that the apparently loathsome sculpture of the Beggar had addressed him, had held him, on his way home from school.

He thrust his plate away from him. The sun shone on the rice. Each grain darkened itself with the shadowy brush of a painter, the grain of things – bone, flesh, glass, wood.

The Beggar's skin was split into tiny holes, into sliced rice and surreptitious vegetables that had been seized secretly by the sun. Loathsome, yes, but possessed of a bright and dark power, of hidden sometimes brilliant eyes.

The holes in the face rifled my son's emotions, they left him with a curious sickness he could not evade or immediately overcome.

It was his first visionary experience (as though the whole world became a parcel of Children) of a true Beggar in the place in which he lived. A Child may see and yet not see the flesh-and-blood mask of a true Beggar that rifles its way through history. Such an experience is unforgettable. It clings to one from the moment one is born (though one forgets) to make and remake one's sensibilities within Time, beyond Time. He had had it. He had forgotten it. Now it returned to become the signal of fate and freedom, the signal of a mother of art associated with the childhood of art which probes into the vision of a creation utterly old, utterly new.

I recall it all now as if the words I use in this narrative (which are set out more vividly, it seems, than anything I may have thought) *are sprung from the spiritual (rather than material) hunger in the log-book of the artist who is my son. Years have passed and I have become a woman of speaking glass or eloquent paper or wood in his Imagination.* That was how I actually felt at the time when he came home, an ageless child of eight, and refused to eat. Helpless as wood yet involved in traces of reflection I scarcely understood. Something stirred the memories of a lost father who had vanished in an ocean of forest. He had vanished yet he remains constant at our table awaiting a new form or visibility. Where is he now? Past and present tenses rush together. What is *now*? Does one regain *now* in works of art that respond to an inconsumable moment, bringing flesh that waits everywhere in uncanny substances into reflected appearances and emotions?

I recall that my son had known poor people but had never seen a Beggar like this before. West Street was not a theatre, it seemed, for such terrible masquerades of history. Was the Beggar Chinese, Portuguese, Spanish, African, Indian? He was one and all of these. He was an unfinished head of state disguised as a forgotten citizen. I accompanied my son back to the corner but the Beggar was no longer there. The neighbourhood was quiet and residential and it was wholly unusual for such beggars to be seen, even if they were there. An astonishing statement perhaps, but that was how I felt.

My son must have been equally irritated at the Beggar's disappearance. He blurted out – 'Do you think,' he cried in a voice like a line of paint, 'that it could be the startling return of my father from the ocean of the forest where he was lost?'

What is memory? I am the mother of an artist. *I have returned in my son's paintings and writings and sculptures to celebrate a sad time for us, as I knew, as he knew.* What is the celebration of a mother's and a son's sadness? What is a homecoming when we scarcely know those who are lost, our alien brothers, sisters, husbands, wives?

What is home, after long years, when we arrive like solid ghosts? Where on Earth or beyond do we arrive? It seemed to me now that some of these visitors, or solid ghosts, as they seemed in my son's art, had been intent on consuming every inch of bread or cake in our home.

Was this an exaggeration of memory or was it the truth of an art that seeks to establish a timeless role for a strange Beggar whose hunger of spirit endures in every material feast?

My husband, his father, my son's father, was scarcely known

to me. He had vanished at an early time, before I knew him well, but he left a sense of stricken happiness which could not be erased. He seemed perfect but elusive.

'Why should he return in such loathsome disguise? Tell me! Tell me! Why such a disguise? Do I not know him? Do you not know him?'

His words were an echo from near and yet from afar. They were a lament I shared with him. *I wanted to know myself as partial (and therefore as striving for fulfilment) and as peculiarly helpless as I felt on the day he was eight, though I was the mother of art. Goddesses of oracle had been assumed to be such mothers but this insight had been wasted or forgotten. He*, the ageless artist, needed to lament the apparently motherless fate of the inexpressible/expressible, inexpressible childhood, inexpressible/expressible maturity. Without such a lament, in works of art, between mother and son, the inexpressible would remain for ever hidden and unborn.

Who was then to say *I* was not a necessary and fertile ghost on the Ship of Art? Thus do I share with him the inexpressible/expressible birth of the Imagination.

I was alive in the shadows of the Imagination and suddenly I was inspired, *in the depths of himself*, to reply to the words he had uttered.

'You know of Odysseus, do you not? He spent long years, after Troy, making his way home by sea. He arrived at long last disguised as a Beggar. His crew, who had been lost or drowned, were alien and invisible then. But did they not lurk in the holes and crevices of his mask? They were unconsciously/subconsciously there. You will find it as well in pre-Columbian, ancient masks, in the oceans of forest of South and Central America, alternative faces secreted in one mask, the faces sometimes of alternative natures whose subtlety we have long forgotten to read. No wonder the Beggar, in one shape or form, endures. Is he the victor disguised? Does he not encompass victims who appear to be conquered or lost or dead?'

'No, no,' he protested, with an air of perverse delight, unconscious delight perhaps, with the close-fitting, infantile, it seemed, biases of humanity; 'Odysseus was the noblest Beggar. Not like this...'

'What is nobility?' I interrupted, spontaneously responding to him with the art of contested consciousness, aroused in curious ways in him and in me. 'The goddess who motivated Odysseus to disguise himself...' I hesitated then continued, '... what did she mean? No one seems able to say what she spiritually intended in a Beggar. And yet *you* have seen the astounding rarity in the disguise of a Beggar despite your addiction to a famous story-line that moves on the surfaces and ignores the subtle openings beneath. Is this rarity not the inexplicable mind of the Imagination, a mind in thrall, nevertheless, to the stubbornness of addicted form the goddess may have sought to question?'

I had no idea where the words came from. *Silent words.* Spoken by *eloquent wood resembling flesh, marked, scarred flesh-in-wood.* I had been sculpted and this brought home to me the acute injuries one inflicted on nature while remaining ignorant of one's responsibility. Was this the implicit intention in works of art that grieved for a language of innate fulfilment *not based on violence* they still inflicted?

Was this the human tragedy or was it the ceaseless, unfinished beginning in which each injury transfigured itself into a hole or corridor between inner man and outer man, between alien man (so-called) and familiar man (so-called)?

I wondered, as I looked back at what I had said, what I meant by 'addicted form'. Did I mean a form of addiction humanity could break or overcome? Or did I mean an addiction so invincible it imposed itself on a humanity that had no inkling it was so gripped in its models and its values? Perhaps it was a mixture of the two. Which was mother, which was son, it was impossible to say.

We lived in West Street, Harbourtown, South America, in 1933. Much time has passed since then. A canal ran between the two promenades of West Street. A tall eucalyptus tree grew in the front of our garden. It is still there after all these years. A sunflower waves at me in a gentle breeze. I stand like a ghost of flesh-in-wood. Years, decades possibly, have passed but everything appears to endure in an inconsumable Moment that sparks and burns on the Beggar's lips. He turns his enigmatic face to me now and I see him through my son's eyes. I see again my son's abstention, his refusal to eat, as though the face of the Beggar appears on his plate. He refuses to eat . . . He will eat, however, sooner or later. The cannibalism of history, which has gripped him like a voter who is unable to vote, will fade. There is a necessity for plain food. But his abstention has created a Moment that undermines the gross, material appetites of the age.

Such grossness turns one's stomach around into a sickness that begins to measure space and time and humanity in new ways. This curious sickness – let us say – of art is the beginning of discoveries of hidden motives and reflexes in conventions we take for granted.

Such sickness brings death and life together in profoundly challenging mosaics and sculptures of seeming flesh which we find in an Egyptian sarcophagus. The mummified king, like sculpted wood, has food beside him. He is supposed to eat but his flesh undergoes a subtle and subconscious change not by satisfying an appetite but by a hunger of spirit that reaches beyond wealth or mummification. *Here is an ancient, hidden motivation we have never considered that runs in the blood-stream of modern sculpted flesh-in-wood.*

Thus it was that I was born or reborn, in the year 2000, to a Beggar whose face on my son's plate led him to extract me in a ghostly sculpture from material, gross pressures that would have kept me underground for ever. Was I the Mother of Art, the Mother of Space? An astounding resurrection. Was I a goddess of oracles and of ambiguity? *I had died in 1952 (according to my son's records) but an inexplicable spirit remained that activated hidden motivations in the life of art.*

My son had left West Street a long time ago and was living now in Water Street beside the great Harbourtown River close to the Atlantic.

I was equipped with a wing for flight. I flew back from 2000 to 1933 to the middle of the nineteenth century when slavery had been abolished in South American Harbourtown and emaciated Africans in my eyes, holes for eyes, had fled the plantations and come to town.

I saw two ghostly ships, the *Lord Elgin* and the *Ulysses*, approaching the harbour on which I stood. It was a map of art. They were bringing Chinese from China, Chinese Immigrants who had crossed an ocean as if they came from one planet to another.

A map of art. Am I the mother (or the Child) of ambiguous creation?

Did I arrive *first*, invisibly first, as the *womb of evolution*, womb of fire, womb of flood? Yet my son has *created* me through holed wood, that becomes my bruised flesh, through glassy knuckles and paint which appear to live, as if to witness to *a conflict of double firsts, double creations, evolution and creation.*

Has he not evolved each doubling word that I write, has he not painted tongues of fire and flood, calm and turbulence, in my mouth?

Is he the first creative god or is he himself caught in a mysterious net in which *first* mother and *first* son come alive again and again beyond themselves in primordial fictions seeking truth?

Thus do I stand as myself, as the Mother of Space, yet made by another on a map of art, by my son who resembles a god, a *creating* god.

I remember the sunflower in the gentle breeze at my home in West Street. That was in 1933. This is in the middle of the nineteenth century, is it not? And yet the sun is blazing on a wave like yellow, fiery blossom in my holed eyes. Is this blaze the universal pointed garden of the sea that brings me inner sight other than a fleshly gaze? Art is the mystery of Spirit.

There is another mystery, the mystery of consciousness, involved in the 'voices' that my son hears in his studio. I died in 1952 and yet I speak in 2000 (after my death) and in 1850 (before my birth). My son claims he hears the real and subtle 'voices' of sculptures and paintings he makes *in himself* and translates them into words and into eloquent paint. Such translations are real and unreal, and they exact penalties. The artist loses his name, he becomes a god, a vulnerable god. Namelessness is founded on multiple names. Multiplicity is Spirit.

2

'What is originality?' a beardless Chinese Boy asked. He seemed beardless in the light of thick, grassy hair on his head. His body was made of glassy, transparent wood with white veins and bones within that seemed to gleam.

'It is rare, it is indefinable,' another replied who stood beside me on the map of art.

There were stiffly wrought figures who were educated to police and to count the Immigrants. Educated! Did education mean an addiction to history on a linear, one-track plane of which none was aware? *Silent words.* I spoke in silences with a tongue of fire in my mouth as every cautious sculpture does. No use courting arrest. Better to think than to speak.

I felt, as I looked around, that there were differences the educated police or establishment entertained about one or two Immigrants such as the beardless Boys on the map. They had been schooled in values. But their school operated on the surface of fact.

Did this explain their stiffness or efficiency to be exercised for the plantations? I could not say. Their values had hardened. Originality had been reduced to Nothingness or to a mere statistic. The beardless Boys had vanished though they stood beside me and were part of my silences. The inner core of fact, its strange hidden openness to new possibilities, remained unseen within an abyss. An abyss of fear, the fear of looking too deep into the origins of a profound, universal understanding.

I felt the clutch of the stiffly wrought figures on my wrist, telling me or my son what to write. But I had been silent, had I not? Had anything been heard? They released me. Was it a release or a caution?

A jumble of thoughts that need to be probed again and again. Many are unaware of the one-sided discourse they follow in discussing events. Others have an inkling but they are silent. Silent as if they are sculpted wood in a work of art. *Yet silences speak in works of art that view the hidden past in depth.* Silences may throw caution to the winds and speak. Then thought itself, that has suppressed itself, and been silent all along, speaks with rare consciousness.

A silent community speaks on surfaces linked to depths, in variations in search of truths we have forgotten.

A painting speaks to a painting.

They speak by crossing chasms. Their frames confine them and make them unnaturally silent. Chasms exist outside each frame, in spaces, in seas, in lands, miniaturized and virtually unseen but with immense and living potential. They fly backwards to one another across each chasm.

What do I mean by *backwards*? I am uncertain but imbued with an eerie confidence extending into realms of Sleep from which long-lost or suppressed consciousness awakens. An uncanny awakening that takes me totally by surprise. The studio in Water Street gives a faint shudder in the bed of land in which it stirs. *Flesh of wood looks up from the streets.* Am I truly one of them now, though I have died? Do I share their life – or progress into death? Do I share their unconscious susceptibility to a measureless art, in an instant of shuddering reality that shakes the Earth to its foundations?

What are Earth's foundations but a faint and turbulent awakening to life we have long suppressed? Is this not the meaning of art?

What do I mean by backwards?

I and they, paintings and sculptures, flesh and wood, in the faint turbulence of the Earth, fly backwards – even if forwards – to greet each other more in the living tissues of the past than in the hollows of the present.

Christ wakes his Mother to bring her back from the Sleep of complacent tradition to life in Byzantine art. A mutual awakening. He holds her in his painted hand like a butterfly of brilliance, a fossil butterfly, a dead brilliance and beauty in painted objects. How does he touch her? How does she live? They cross a chasm, of which we need to learn, that lies outside of frames of culture which art engenders and passes through to achieve a *measureless* equality between peoples and races.

Such originality cannot be seized as a literal text. It is a single penetration of the tapestry of Silence which makes two instant holes with which to hear what the other says, it is a single brushstroke that makes two instant paintings with a miniature but immense chasm between divisions of paint. *It is the quantum miracle,* Sleep and Awakening. Mother and Son become equals though diverse in their roles of a creating god, taxed to extremity, and a mother of art or symbolic sculpture and painting of flesh. They speak for me and my son within parallels of difference and engagement across seas and lands. They speak for an imperilled Mankind divided in itself without an appreciation of the chasms they should cross to find the origins of life.

A muffled music came up to the studio from the streets, abusive, stiff, gentle, sensitive, repulsive, violent, fearful . . . It flooded the large, echoing studio. A muffled, inexplicable tongue in the throat of 1850. A chorus of contradictions from which we needed to learn how to make crossings from violence to gentleness in the arts enveloping wooden Mankind.

My son listened and was held by the voices of the sculptures in the streets. Fearful voices. He was immersed in a time for which but a frail tissue of statistics existed. What were they fearful of? Was it a faint shuddering...? Fear was strong in the violent chorus – as it seemed – that rose from the streets. Fear of happenings unreal now, in 2000, but acutely true in 1850. So true and real the voice of fleshly wood in the streets seemed to break its frame and mould and to become strangely – perhaps subconsciously – alive. The tissue of statistics waved like a frail curtain of fire in the streets and in the room. Nothing was burnt in 2000 but the fear of fire made a burning threat accessible to all beneath the level of consciousness.

Within the frail curtain he had created my son saw the *Lord Elgin* and the *Ulysses* rise from the sea into Harbourtown port. They were built of blocks of transparent fire, so frail, so non-existent they seemed, it was impossible to tell why such fear, such panic, broke into the room. Was it the painted survival of fire in water, in the sea, in the ocean?

Such paint was impossible except in the renascence of the ancient in the modern. Were the Ships figures of suppressed Imagination – long buried in and long before 1850 – rising now from the Sea and appearing so real, so shudderingly true, they brought terror to all who came brokenly alive at that moment? Water dripped from fire across a chasm and made the sculptures in the streets sing or speak in muffled tones within the responsive studio linking the streets to each grain or pattern that ran along walls or floors or windows.

I stood now with echoing voice in Water Street. Was I the voice of the streets on a map of art? Or had I come alive though made to seem alive? What distinction is there between a seeming, material life in a frame that dies, or is made to die, and a true, inner life that speaks across each grain? I touched my son's walking stick, his knife, his brush, his pen. An airy touch that left them as they were, burning yet not burning, in his hand.

What is art? What knowledge do we truly have of implements that tell us of the riddles of the past?

A Ship of fire, a Pen or Brush of fire, fire that is not fire, may be an atmospheric trick or it may tell of furies, modulated, toned down, on planet Earth. It may tell of Venus that is an unbearable furnace in the Sky. Venus exists across distances from Earth we do not *psychically* understand. Such distances are close in psyche and yet faraway as a frail sunflower bobbing and burning on a wave. How close is China to South America, how far away from each other are these planetary waving continents in an Ocean of Space?

Is inner peace the material benign raised into complacent hardness – where we are pulled into explosions of the Self in one another – or is it a voyage into spiritual deprivations we have amassed that bring us back to contemplate a corridor in the Beggar's mask that remains a subtle opening into the origins of meaning within the tone and temper of the furies?

I was the Mother of Space and I found myself, sparse of detailed wholeness of the radial or non-radial tree of evolution as I was, holed of tongue as I was, speaking to my son in the chimes of a Clock that seemed to come from everywhere and nowhere. It came from above. It came from below. Was it a single chime, a dual chime, congregating into many? It came from a Tower, it seemed, at the end of Water Street. The street glistened into holes under a sheet of metallic water. The chime or chimes struck its face as well. Floods and holes were frequent in Water Street that suffered from the great Harbourtown River and from the tides of the ocean. The chiming spirit of Space, its height and depth, seemed now my inner voice, my water voice, my Tower voice. My son picked up my voice, in a vestigial Moment, in a hunger of spirit, and painted it on my tongue. He sought to test the hole, or two holes instantaneously punctured there, with a miniature bell within resembling the Clock at the end of the Street. The Clock also stood elsewhere in the room, within my airy reach, twisted and torn as if hit by a storm. My son listened deeply to the chords in himself. He wrote instantaneously what I said in his Notebooks. Two Clocks or chimes were written and drawn in letters of art, *they were instantaneously aroused from one penetration of Space*, in the Mother of Space. I was looking proudly at his Ship that plastered another wall. It sailed towards me even as it bounced to a standstill in the room. I spoke of it now with my holed tongue that echoed the quantum movement and station in a work of art.

'Why do you not show your Chinese friends of the twentieth century your idea of how their antecedents came to South America? Why do you not show them the reflected body of your feeling, the Silences in you that speak through me, the quantum holes of consciousness through which art lives . . .?'

He stared at me and shook his head. 'Impossible,' he said.

'Why?' I asked. 'Why impossible?'

'Impossible,' he repeated. 'Their antecedents have arisen from the Sea. Who would believe this? They have broken through the Beggar's mask. Who would accept that? Do you not see? The Beggar's face is a series of delicate waves.' He was pointing to an unfinished painting half-hidden behind the map of art. '*He* has changed, is still changing. *They* have changed, are still changing. Has their consciousness of a collective change, embracing the world, *come alive*? I do not think so. Do you not see?' He addressed me partly in anger, partly in grief, as though he spoke through me to the inmost rising mystery of consciousness in himself.

I stared with my holed eyes and I saw what I had not fully

seen before. I saw how lonely he was, how alone, how *conscious* of being alone. Such consciousness reached nevertheless into the beginnings of Space, into items one took for granted as symbolically alone and forever stranded in material, fragmented structures. I saw a lonely, painted Clock, twisted and torn, yet speaking through me, a lonely sculpture. A staggering possibility that shook me and made me come close to crumbling and falling even though I had been aware of my life in art before. Such an awareness was tormenting in its acute deprivation of a spiritual, whole understanding. I saw the burning Ship, which was not burning at all, as lonely as a lighthouse arisen from the bottom of the Sea, I saw the Sea in the Beggar's face with holes in the waves of disguise through which the changed and changing Immigrants came unconscious or subconscious of true change.

Had my son dipped his Brush in the furies?

There they were. The Immigrants came ashore in two groups. One group came from the *Lord Elgin*. That group seemed *not to have drowned at all* in the massive Sea that edged the walls of the room in which I stood. The other group, from the *Ulysses, were the drowned ones*, secreted in, but emerging from, the Beggar's universal, waving disguise. It had been a hard crossing, a week seemed a year, two months became *psychical* ages in the depths of the storm-tossed, Clock-driven waters. And yet the *Ulysses* group, emaciated as they were in my holed eyes, were solid and real works of art. They had been created within *tensions* not only of numinosity and hazardous evolution but of line and being that gave them a subtle independence or consciousness of freedom. The others, from the *Lord Elgin*, who were apparently alive, seemed ghosts, unreal phantoms of the past. It was with difficulty that they survived with presence in a 2000 work of art. Apparently living yet inwardly destined to die in a reversal of all subtle independence or consciousness in their structure. How else could I put it? Was this a tension in my son's art between oblivion in ornamentation and inner, unfinished truth to which I clung?

Was this a way of defeating the stiffly drawn policing establishment who still counted, as if they had nothing else to do, each parcel of Immigrants?

What did they count? I looked as closely as I could at the work of art with all its ambiguities and tensions. Did they count shells for sale or for prison that they saw – on the surface of existence, without further thought – as ornamented or ornamental flesh-and-blood?

Flesh-and-blood. Ornament. Two holes, deceptive and revealing, in the tapestry of Space: so close together now that they did not seem to be quantum holes at all, *in me, or anyone else*, but a block, a single, material vision, hiding scrupulously (or unscrupulously) the running lines of dialogue in art between Spirit and life. *Yet those lines were there* in the *Ulysses* group ascending from the Sea on feet that blundered, did not run but walked.

I saw their deprivations, their blunders, in myself, as Mother of Space, but I knew the lines of originality were there that the policing establishment counted without seeing until they vanished out of existence.

My son touched the holes for eyes and for tongues in me, vision and speech were different, yet they translated each other into formless Silences.

What are Silences in the art of sculpture? Is sculpture form and formlessness in its reach, in its open potency? It was a question I could never wholly answer. Is sculpture a diversification of painting that slides into bodily being? I would come to it, as the eruptive mystery of consciousness, again and again.

'They heard the Clock in the waves of the Sea,' my son

cried. He was translating 'Clock' into 'waves'. 'They heard the Clock in the waves but they have forgotten the translations of reality as they blunder ashore, the blundering arts of the drowned. *That is how I see them now at the end of the twentieth century. That is how I paint and sculpt them. You* remember, do you not? I bring them ashore like Immigrants who arrive from a distant planet, which is translated into peculiar, vulnerable conditions they must learn to understand in themselves. They have travelled across Space, they have truly changed. They reside (yet no longer reside as I see them) in the Beggar's spiritual disguise and mask. An impossible but true myth. A universal, secretly holed mask, corridors out of the Sea.'

He looked at me almost helplessly. I was startled. Had I come from the Sea? Did the holes of eye and tongue in me bear a resemblance to the Beggar's Mask? Had I forgotten? The Clock at the end of Water Street seemed to open itself and to strike again, resonating with storm-tossed spaces.

He broke out of his helplessness then and addressed me again from the aloneness of his art.

'How can I paint the chimes of an open Clock that run in the Sea in echoing colours, echoing holes that breathe and listen, *without a collective Memory,* frail perhaps but collective nevertheless, *in you, in the Mother of Space,* whom I sculpt and paint into independent being? *Consciousness beyond me, in me, as I work and create, is my master and mistress.* What am I saying, what am I doing? I am alone and helpless.' He stopped, astounded by the contradictions in need of translations, collective Memory (which he desired), alone and helpless (as he confessed). He went on as if seeking a translation of sorts in the Beggar's mask. 'Here is the Homeric hero of ancient epic. Is he not alone and helpless as Time accumulates? All heroes are. *Now,* in this Moment, he reveals a hunger of Spirit we never suspected that releases us in an organ of unpredictable creation.'

He paused; then continued: '*You* must know. *You are the bride and the mother of the Beggar.*'

I could scarcely give credit to what he had said. Then I blurted out in voices that rose from Water Street: '*No, no*, it is not true, not true at all.' A man and a woman were quarrelling in the Street and their voices stumbled in my ears.

He conceded within himself: 'Not *literally* true. *Numinously true.* You lost your husband, my father, soon after I was born. Do you know him? Would you recognize him? He vanished in a Sea of Forest. You think of him as perfection. You told me so as a Child. Perfection, you said. What is perfection? It becomes for you and for me a *staggering* loss. I do not know my father. It takes me back into the dark ages of the universe where so much is lost. It takes you back . . . These' – he pointed to the Immigrants who had arrived from the burning Ship, burning like a lighthouse in Space, and were mixed into the voices below – 'come ashore and blunder into your arms as sons of water and blood. Transparency marries blood and is translated in you into a mother of staggering losses from which you gain a measure of true creation, an organ of creation. Out of such losses comes an organ. Do you not see?'

'Not I,' I said blindly. 'I do not see.'

I was the one who should have seen.

'Not you alone. I gain too. All humanity does. Who are humanity's ancestors? Lost ancestors in the dark ages . . . Or a *single* ancestor equally lost, for ever lost, except within an organ of true creation that ceaselessly returns. Do you not see? Chinese, Europeans, Indians, Africans, Incas, Aztecs and others I find difficulty in naming, blunder into the arms of the Mother of Space, the Bride of Space. That is how I see you *now, living* sculpture, *living* painting. Do you not see yourself?'

He stopped and stared at me from within himself, a withinness that reached beyond himself into me and beyond me. I still refused to accept myself as the Mother and the Bride of the Beggar. And yet I felt I began to know how he had arrived at such a precarious identity of opposites, such a precarious art of collective Memory in me, in my apparently isolated, apparently trivial experiences in a corner of South America. Nothing is trivial in a hunger of Spirit that gains numinous figures of Space from incredible material losses that, on their own, could make us into prisoners of race.

Had he seized me, I wondered, as part-death, part-life, partial death, partial life? *I died in 1952.* Strange to tell of one's death except in a partial tongue one borrows from an artist or a god who *learns* of Silence in formless, if not Timeless, degrees of the arts.

Such learning never ceases. It is death's gift to life. *It is an organ of music that plays wordlessly, in death and in life, yet it sparks chimes and sounds and murmurs in waters, lands and trees, in everything, and in the contradictory voices of theatre and opera.*

It all began when my son accepted the death of a mother as appropriate for rituals that perceived freedom from a mother as circumstantially right for a son. But an unease existed in his works of art, an unease that tied them to the ground and left them insensitive (if not wholly insensible) to the *murmur* of flood or to curtains of fire. In the ritual death of his mother my son became curiously aware of the traditional passing of oracles once exercised by women called goddesses. So long ago this had been that the exercise had become a numb archetype or had faded in male properties, in male rule, into virtual non-existence. How could he paint or sculpt such non-existence without the gift of death, dead archetype, dead rule, that lived nevertheless in the ground of art?

There was his mother, on the one hand, and on the other a

dim figure of Space providing a gap or vacancy behind or within the Beggar's Mask.

Could that gap or vacancy be translated into a key in the doors of corridors of legend?

The dim figure began to strengthen in the ground of insensitive achievement and to emerge into better, creative view.

Not simply as an individual mother but as a potent recall of oracles of Space beyond a ritual language. He felt the powers of the key of Space, long forgotten, long discarded, by static codes. He communed with this growing figure that brought such gifts. He heard it turn and bow in the surges of the Ocean, in Clocks, in a confused clamour that rose from the streets of Harbourtown. *Such gratings of the key, the sweetest, most demanding key,* became louder in Water Street where he had established a new studio.

These were the beginnings of partial death, partial life, mutual archetype, in all the sculptures and paintings he made as if he were becoming a god in his creation of a goddess. Did art *run* in the hands of a man who substituted himself for an unknowable Creator through Mothers and Brides of Space?

Such questions he had never asked of anyone before. *Now* they came with a force he had not imagined. He visited 1933 all over again and listened to his mother speaking again of the Beggar he had seen in West Street.

A loathsome face the Beggar possessed as though arisen from the womb of a grave. Brilliant eyes nevertheless flaring at times like stars when night falls. He listened to what the oracle of a mother said to him all over again. The Beggar, she said, was the legend of ancient Odysseus in disguise. Why had it come again? What did it mean? What new thing did it bring and announce? It was alone. It had travelled for years that seemed to run into centuries. Its crew had vanished, all drowned in the Sea. 'It' and 'he' were translations of subtle, enormous difference in every legend...

Son and man and god and artist were a Child when she spoke to him, like a Child herself, in 1933, but so gripped was he in the Beggar's waving disguise his foot moved on to a perilous path...

She sought to relieve him of the sickness from which he suffered, his refusal to eat what appeared to be the Beggar's broken skin in his meal. A broken materialism that still seemed whole to many who could not read the fissures in their story-line legends.

The Mask of the Beggar began to suffer a new and terrifying translation that would lead him into many re-appraisals of complacent tradition. It extended itself across years, centuries, ages. It opened itself into unsuspected corridors in a Sea of Space. Its brilliant eyes spoke of mirrors that could lead the drowned back home. Where is home when one has ventured on the Sea? The drowned of all cultures around the world began to arrive in South America. Who were the drowned? This was a question that would activate the undercurrents and the surfaces of his art. *Who were the drowned?* They were all those he sought to create anew. They had never truly arrived, whatever they may have thought. Only *now* they saw themselves arriving, in blundering flesh-and-blood, swimming in Space that made them sensitive to groundings they had never understood.

He took his cue from the music of Space exercised now by an oracle he perceived in resemblances to his mother. It was a cue that reflected his mother's lost husband, *his* father, whom she portrayed as perfection. Astonishing perfection in realms of sickness.

It all began on a Day he sought to catch afresh in his art. Mother and Bride and Oracle. The year 1933 came timelessly alive in 2000 and 1850 as signals of times that had accumulated into deprivations. Save for a precarious Oracle that brought him on the threshold of a collective Memory he would need to probe and to seek again and again.

Yes, I knew he had seized me as partial death, partial life, in the ramifications of his art. I knew how he had come to visualize me as Bride and Mother within/beyond hazardous recollections of the Beggar and of all those who come now through fissures of legend into true existence. I saw it all but I could not accept it. Did he accept it? Was he not uncertain still in the creation of his live paintings and sculptures? They were alive for him and for me, but could I be entirely free of the god who makes me? It did not seem so. His uncertainties would tincture my being within subjective independence.

Yet despite uncertainties I felt a shiver run through my wooden/fleshly limbs. Did wood become flesh in a quantum instant? I had changed. Did I remember the forests from which I came? Were they forests or deserts or grassy valleys that had undergone tumultuous, mutual, unrecorded ages? Ancient forests under a Sea of Space. Ancient wood sensitized into the flesh of art in waving ground on which I stood.

There was a Chinese woman holding an arm of mine where I stood on the map of art. I was astonished. She had been placed there surreptitiously, I thought, by the artist or god who was my son. I felt I knew the reason for such a surreptitious approach. I protested: 'There were no women on the *Lord Elgin* or the *Ulysses*. All men. Eighty or ninety men on each vessel. China was in a turmoil. A series of wars and battles. The Immigration laws in Harbourtown in the mid-nineteenth century were designed to bring labour quickly from one planetary continent to another. Labour was in absolute demand. You wish to deceive me. And that is why you have put her so quietly, so secretly, on my arm. I should not feel a thing since my arm is made of wood, fleshly-seeming though it may be.'

'Do you not see *in yourself and others* that life was cheap, is cheap?'

'Cheap!' This had taken me, taken him, it seemed, by surprise.

He stared at me with his helpless, wandering look that roamed around the large studio and room of magical consciousness.

'We may pretend otherwise,' he said at last, 'but if we're honest it is clear that life is cheap in many areas of the world outside of the frames we maintain. Framed pictures, aren't they? Many ways of seeing such frames with Imagination... That is why I bring you to *her*' – he pointed to the woman on my arm – 'as someone who cannot be contained in the closures and statistics and records. She came on the *Ulysses*. She disguised herself as a Boy, a beardless Boy. I need your deepest reflections on the changes that happened to her, somewhat forgotten changes no doubt, upon a great Sea of Space. No record or statistic tells us of these. I see statistics very often as curtains of fire threatening to destroy... You need to *listen* beyond yourself, within yourself, to what she has to say.'

'How can I listen? She will say what you want her to say.'

He was staring at me as helplessly as ever.

'If art is simply what the artist wishes to say,' he said at last, 'then we are lost. There is such a thing as freedom of character in a novel or a poem or a painting. It has virtually disappeared, I know, and that makes for easy reading, easy seeing. *You* must know of elements of subjective, surprising independence in art. Such elements bear on the reality of consciousness. Who knows truly what consciousness is? This is a formidable and I would think open matter. If it goes entirely into a closure, if it does not entertain alternatives in speech, in vision, then – as I said before – we are quite lost. We are framed for ever, each racial or cultural frame does unconsciously what the other does. No crossing of chasms. Violence rules.'

The woman on my arm was passive, her skin was the colour of Sky and Rain. What could I make of such passivity? Then I was fired by silent grief within the passive contours of her flesh. It was astonishing, it left me confused, amazed. The passivity of her features seemed incongruous with fire and grief but it was not. I studied her eyes which were the colour of Rain and saw through them – the way she glanced in them and through them – a reflection of her husband's look as he stood on the map behind me. Each glance she gave became a day, a week, a month, a year. Time was compressed in her eyes. At nights she seemed to disappear but with the dawn she was back on my arm. I studied her afresh with each light and began to see her husband more clearly or starkly than before. There was a print on his chest: SHANG DYNASTY. He stood comparatively close to her. They were apart by feet, by a yard, by yards, no more, but he seemed to stand in China, as though he had never left, whereas she was here, she had arrived. It took me by storm and I remembered the storm-tossed Clock of the Sea.

Was she crying, was she weeping? The Rain in her eyes did not fall into tears. I too was unable to bring tears to the holed sockets of my eyes. But within the passivity of her glance I knew a wealth of crying that flooded the room. The *Ulysses* had arisen in blocks of closed histories burning indestructibly, however faintly, into open legend. It had arisen from the bottom of the Sea where it sailed unseen in its drowned state as if on the crest of a wave. Drowned vessels are never seen until it is too late. It had arisen now, however, and it brought her into the room without tears that went deeper than the tears I thought I knew.

I was still confused, amazed. Not a word had she spoken but I heard her voice as clear as a bell ringing in my ears, ringing in the waves. She had arrived after a journey that brought her through deceptive and revealing spaces in layers that seemed the same though they were not. The fires of Ocean had given a passivity to her glance, her flesh had changed, her body, her being, all had changed with each touch of a god who seemed subterranean and ageless and who placed her on my arm and made me see into myself, and my passive crying, the crying of a silent rage of consciousness.

I needed to study her much more closely but at the moment I was held by what I saw at the back of the room through her eyes.

Her husband had bought a shop in which he sold vegetables, sugar, rice, potatoes, plantains, salt-fish, meat and fruit. Huge papaws and mangoes were on sale. Clothing also draped a wall of the shop like sculpted bodies marching in and out of Space.

There was a door to a back room. The door was half-open now. The room was like a cave. He assembled his friends there in the evenings. They gambled, dice and cards. Had he brought China and crossed the Ocean with it in a dream of a cave?

The woman on my arm gave a scream. 'He is wounded,' she said in a loud voice that sought a form of help.

'Wounded!' I cried instantly. 'Where is he wounded?'

And then I was lost in a deeper amazement. How had I spoken? How had she? All previous answers to such questions seemed to fall away. I had entered a different chasm or void. She spoke Chinese in the Silences of her life. I knew not a word in Chinese. An illumination flashed out of her passive frame. Was it a mirror flashing Sun from the Street? She had screamed and spoken as if it were a prayer to the Sun. Was it a prayer to the Mother of Space whose arm she held? *As such I had replied instinctively and instantly in accord with a flare of Sun.*

Prayers to gods, who were sons of the Mothers of Space, were made by the million every second, every minute, in every glance of an eye. How can gods respond to such an unearthly clamour of visions and appeals? The gods are overwhelmed. Easy enough perhaps to perceive one's prayer, in a particular language, as outweighing every other. My Imagination was fired. A sharp and terrible responsibility arose. *I* had been approached by the woman on my arm. Not a god. *She* had spoken to me directly.

'Where is he wounded?' My question came instantly in response to her scream. Two holes of strangest dialogue between a Chinese and a non-Chinese in the tapestry of Space. One was her cry, silent but loud, the other a quantum immediate response, involving signals in Space, to be weighed, considered, translated, if necessary, into uncertain equivalents.

Had I sensed, however remotely, through her passive frame, a way in which an unknowable God absorbs the multiple languages of prayer?

Art was a substitute through which one was involved, whether as a goddess or a god, to respond to multiple cries in the Silences of a numb humanity of wood or glass or flesh. Whatever divisions one made, whatever philosophical calculations, none were to be taken literally.

'Look at his hands,' she said. 'Tell me how wounded he is.' I made no reply but she understood I was looking into a formless Spirit we shared in our helplessness, in our passivity, on a map of art.

I had become aware of an acute sensation within her. This related to the Wound on her husband's hands that I still could not discern. We were tied together and all I could do was wait for deeper clarification of an imponderable issue. I saw that the hands were intent now on leaving the cave that they had brought with them from China. I saw this out of the corner of my eye. One's holed eyes gave one an extra darkness, an extra light, through which one saw the accumulating terrors of the world. Deprivations, perhaps I should say, through which one learnt the grain of a measureless Wisdom in breaking formalities and complacencies.

Where were the hands? Yes, there they were. They came towards her by shadowy, painted design like a fleet of cards willing itself to reach her. *Will* was a *tool* I had never seen in this light before. *Hands* were a *tool*. I was dumbfounded by such findings and by a combination of signals I needed to weigh ceaselessly that came out of helplessness on the map of art. Was the world more one-sided and helpless than it accepted in its technological traditions?

Was this an aspect of the Wound to which I was being drawn?

The hands I saw out of a corner of my eye were indeed a general's or an admiral's tool divorced from the voyage that its wife had made in her sensitivity. A sensitive passivity beyond marriage to a tool. A sensitive art. They (the hands that were a tool) scouted for such sensitivity they did not truly value, as if they sought to make her into a lifeless, betting resource for a battle they still had to fight. The high, painted Seas around us were a battlefield or a gambling table. Harbourtown itself shook in a tremor of her arm on mine. Gambling was an addiction of which I had no doubt. I saw the hands coveting Spanish dice on the floor, floating on the Seas, French, Dutch, British, Russian dice as they crossed the room towards her. They had been carefully painted and sliced, they had swiftness and agility. I sensed terror or deprivation in her eyes.

Shadowy as they appeared, uniform Shadow that they wore like a transparent glove, each stage, each panel, each disc in a hand had been consummately and vividly executed with an artist's Knife or Pen or Brush. Knife and Brush were as alive and dangerous as the flesh they made. An extraordinary complexity. No, it was quite ordinary. Extraordinary/ordinary. Art cannot avoid violence in its portrayal of numb tools and events. But it sees itself differently. As humanity surrenders itself into a partial tool, will, hands, brain, each separate and existing on its own genetic order, art has to break life into Wounds that have a different meaning.

And still I could not tell exactly what the Wound was that brought such terror to the woman on my arm and to myself. I was deeply affected by her emotion. I looked around at the sculptures and paintings and the writings on wall or floor or paper. I detected lines written by the god or artist in a Notebook as though I heard his speaking thoughts or he heard mine as he sculpted, painted and made me record everything I said.

Was it the Wound of self-made genius in a painting, a Wound that opens itself of its own accord to unsuspected vistas and forgotten influences or alien antecedents in flesh or art?

China and Chinese values were not her sole ancestry.

Had she sensed this when she crossed the Ocean?

Had she sensed that she herself could be ancestral to a foreign painter in the life that was unceasing in his paintings?

The room was darkening now and she vanished at this moment filled with fear that seemed to triumph over her ecstasy in sensing a new vitality of far-flung inner and outer relationships. The god or artist who wrote the lines I had read in myself in his Notebook may have removed her from my arm. He had done so stealthily. He wished to patch the terror we both now felt in one another. The room grew darker still. Lights from the Street below shone in the dark. They picked up hidden contours of bright Day, they revealed lines I had never seen before, they revealed *her* antecedent influence in a run of lines that sparked into being on the floor. She perceived Japanese and Chinese designs threaded into the painting that I now saw for the first time in my life. My holed eyes glittered in astonishment. She perceived her designs, her Chinese designs. Were they hers, or were they to be associated with a hidden treasure belonging to Animal and Spirit and Man? It was there in the waves of Space which she remembered, as in a Dream, as she descended into the waters, flew like a flying fish, in crossing the Ocean. It was a memory of conversions of the Self, of latencies beneath passivity, half-ecstasy, half-terror, half-death, half-life.

The lights from the Street shone and broke into fiery, pointed wings of grass in the hands that groped for her in the waves of the Sea into which she had descended, part-fish, part-flight, part-ghost, part Dream. Wings of grass had been lit in the flesh of the Seas' hands that had become his. Grass in which a bird nestled had become points of fire in a wave. Active now in the Dark as though he had been stung by the subtle beak of the bird or the fin of the fish that had turned into a furnace of greed in a gambler's meditation.

Had he (his Seas' hands) caught her and taken her away? Was he awakening to himself now as he had never done before? Was she in his suddenly awakening grasp? The dice and cards shone like black birds above the hidden bird in the grass, they were Ships of War upon a field.

It was a remarkable, unsuspected capture of Harbourtown that opened from frames of Spain, France, Holland, Britain into the gamble in a cave brought by Chinese Immigrants to South America.

'Where is the Wound?' I cried.

'It's in my quantum painting of the ghost of Van Gogh,' the artist replied. 'I bring him in the shoes of others from Holland who dreamt the Sun and the Night were theirs. They captured Harbourtown and ruled it throughout the eighteenth century until the British won the game and took it early in the nineteenth. She walks with him at the bottom of the Sea where he wears his forgotten Chinese dress. She is afraid of him as well. He has elements that remind her of her husband. I broke the boundary by which he was confined. My quantum painting. Do you see it? She does. The Dutch imperialists once owned Harbourtown. They treated her like a lifeless mistress or a whore. We speak of places in the feminine gender, do we not?'

'The Dutch? Van Gogh was Dutch.'

'Yes, the Dutch. Van Gogh's genius opens at the end of his life and tells two tales, one of which we have framed into an absolute, the other in Sun and Light and Dark tells of travel beyond Europe we do not understand. Save that it may open now into a gamble on the High Seas. The Dutch took Harbourtown from the French, the French captured it from the Spanish. It's a well-known pattern of history. The Chinese came, wholly undistinguished Immigrants, in the middle of the nineteenth century, half-conscious and unconscious of what they were doing, and brought such species of capture to an end.'

There was a sudden Silence. His voice died but stirred again in a clamour from the Street: 'They have caught her. They have sold her.'

'Caught whom? Sold whom?'

'Her husband put her up as a gambling stake. What a stake she was. It's an illness that plagues the world. Everyone at the table became inordinately eager. Whether women were plentiful or few this was a prize to be won. Flesh. Land. Both equally passive. The game turned blinding as it always does. Harbourtown floated as though it were at sea. It was here, it was there. It bounced with every card as if the cave in which they played had split into many ships. Everyone was driven by a centuries-old addiction. *He* had lost his shop, everything in it, and he felt this was his golden chance to win it all back. *But he lost. And then he knew she was real as the waters he had never explored rose around him.* Would you say she became his true wife then? He lifted his hand as if to bless... *He* knew the passivity he had imposed on her, he knew a quality of art one imposes on everything one thinks one possesses.'

A sudden explosion rocked the room. Was it the Sun that had fired into broad daylight? Or was it Venus? Or the furies? Then I saw the Wound through which I had read of the capture of Harbourtown from the Spanish and the French and the Dutch and the British.

'He shot himself,' said the god and artist in the room. 'He understood the crime he had committed. He shot himself before he had signed her away to her new governor. He lies on the floor of the cave at the bottom of the Sea with a hole in his head. Van Gogh's reflective bullet in the imperial flaring Sun that lights my quantum painting.'

Day visited the room in Water Street and Harbourtown. Day danced into a long visit. Painted dancing weeks, months, even years on a rare canvas of Sky. Time seemed more than Time, less than Time, in my holed eyes that looked across distances into visible and invisible stars. Day was Night, Night was Day in my holed eyes.

The visible stars were holed stations such as mine in the room in which I stood, the invisible gave corridors through the holes in the visible, material stations and exposed the vulnerability of creative tumult. Such tumult was extreme and virtually unimaginable but it offered proportions that could be scaled down and modulated into human art as a true nerve and universe of compassion.

I looked at myself in the room in which I stood through a Wound in myself. I was stationary, a piece of sculpture with holes, even as I visited Day and Night in the Sky and saw myself in the dance of creation.

The Art of Journeying from planet to planet in continents on Earth implied a Wound through which I had seen the fleet of Ships from Spain, Holland and Britain. I had seen them as a supreme caution in the wake of events against the capture of Harbourtown. I saw them in a creation of chasms and unbound premises that needed to be understood beyond stationary travel that brings its cave of invulnerable illusion and habit across an Ocean.

Could we, I wondered, relate ourselves to the stars in a supreme modulation of terrifying furies, that are in ourselves and in Space, and provide corridors into lands and waters within art's communion with the living and the dead?

The woman had returned and she leaned once again on my arm. I saw through her eyes into the shape of her husband lying half-in-the-Sky, half-in-the-Sea. She communed with him, in this precarious constellation, Earth and Sky, within the distant tremor of her limbs, I felt, as I looked into Space and saw her apart from absolute passivity. He too seemed other than himself, more than himself, less than himself. Did he not stand in a trembling, self-bitten distance, parts of himself seeming on display, more, less, Earth, Sky? An inner bullet of fury had sliced him. She saw this as clearly as the Sun in my eyes. It was a portent she could not dismiss. She would need to analyse it deeply as she sailed on the Forests of South

America. It made her tremble in anticipation of nameless emotions that would address her.

This was a New World. Was it dying, was it dead, despite its newness, was it potentially alive? Nothing was stationary as it seemed. Her passivity was turning into a mirror through which the profoundest, uncertain movements in nature were revealed.

What is art? Does art provide secretly, with originality, the regeneration of a grasping, self-killing humanity? One kills others in oneself with a bullet that one fires through one's head. One confesses to collective guilt that could be traced around the world since wounded Time began, since the furies began. And yet in that Wound a corridor remains in which one sees oneself, or others see one, precariously, immaterially whole . . .

One heals oneself with a groping knowledge of dancing parts in Space to be encompassed in ceaseless garments of the Sky and Earth.

Was she, the woman on my arm, the Bride of Space? I was astonished at the question I asked myself. A secret, genderless question that the artist or god in the room asked of himself. Was *he* a *Bride* . . . ? No, I was the reflection of the Bride of Space. I was learning her anguish – the anguish of a broken, divided humanity I rarely considered – that was so deep it almost repelled me. I was learning the edges of an ecstasy, so overwhelming it threatened to drown me in a Sea of despair. There is a paradox in ecstasy which we can scarcely bear. I began to feel her pain, the pain of humanity, as if it were wholly mine. *We shared a Brideship beyond name or nature.* Was this a unitary, however elusive, link between us? Brideship of Space, Mothership of Space. The notion of a *Ship* seemed a tool but a tool of such rare sensitivity it extended from our wasting hands and holed bodies like a Brush capable of painting modulations of the furies and of bringing illuminations of the dangers besetting us in the inner and outer Journeys on which we were engaged.

With an inner hand she named the brow of the shape – in which she perceived her dead husband – Shang Mountain or Brow. He was dead, shot flesh, yet his Brow was alive in the Forest. Such is the mystery of art, the mystery of danger, the mystery of *unconscious* hope.

I felt her touch on my head as the artist tenderly moved his Knife or Brush as if seeking to hear words from her or from me.

Such words which he heard – as if they came from the entire room – brought her husband alive, it seemed, within the constellation arising from the Sea.

Art moved a tooled body and made it arise into living land within the Forest.

He had had a print: SHANG DYNASTY on his vest. It was but a vague reminder of times ancient, long past and forgotten, that had touched each other across the Seas through related civilizations – a relationship in which art itself appeared to forget the life of the Brush or the Knife that had carved and painted us into existence. No one remembered the feel of the Knife that turned hard and cool as a gun. Yes, a collective gun with which to fire at each other from impregnable-seeming, secure-seeming fortresses. Each step that we took fell away into another loss, another lost civilization, each Word that we spoke into another vanquished language save for the Beggar's formless visionary speech through cracks or crevices translated into tongues. *Did the memories of all this exist in pre-Columbian South America?* The artist made a Note in his Book.

I saw the sadness in his face. He was a substitute god. He was a substitute for an unknowable Creator. This unknowable Creator or God hovered invisibly over god or gods. I sensed his distress, as I had sensed the pain, the ecstasy, the despair in the woman he had placed on my arm. Universal emotion it was, universal creativity between sculptor and sculpted, painter and painted, writer and written. No character was absolutely controlled by a substitute creator. *There lay a grain of hope.* Consciousness – however diverse in its formal applications – was a universal, spatial entity, a small-seeming entity perhaps yet boundless, unbound.

Would he make Space into the many-sided, largely unknown body of the Immigrant who had fired instinctively at himself as the Knife turned into a gun? Was it a dead man's gun, was it all living men's gun?

Was the Immigrant an unknown version of the Beggar, an unknown version of my Husband? I was a Mother of Space and my son was a substitute god.

He began to trace a network of semi-technological, semi-human pathways from Shang Mountain in the high interior. They ran along the body of Space, the skin of Space, the skin of the Beggar, the skin of the dead Immigrant who had appeared – I now realized – unobtrusively, surprisingly, from a crevice in the Beggar's skin, a crevice in the Sky as much as in the Earth.

Series of rivers like fingers of Space ran from shoulders and arms. Each finger – I was astonished to find – was divided into two. One – an exquisitely sliced narrow and deep river-finger – stood high above Harbourtown, in the far interior, whereas the other – seemingly large but incapable of sustaining a whole flood-current brought by rains from above – was tied to the fortress of Ocean against Harbourtown itself on the coast below. Each sought, in some degree, to compensate for tribal deficiencies in the the body of Space.

A fortress, however strong, has its meaningful fissures. Their depth and their range are blocked but open to the creative eye. Every rock, high and apparently immune above, has its station and invisible movement. It is stationary yet in conserving the flooded reaches of a river it moves invisibly into tidal projections. The fortress of Ocean far below breaches itself into a moving escalation of seeming-rocks that partially release and partially hold the waters upon them.

A marvellous, unconsidered vulnerability – until now in the artist's tracery – that reveals breached fortress and invisibly moving rock to keep the Spirit of the waters in flow in the body of Space.

How could he lean, I wondered, on an Immigrant, who had shot himself, save that there was a mystery in the body of Space? He imitated me in some curious transfigurative way of art I did not understand. I leaned on the woman he had placed on my arm. The Beggar had changed into properties and personalities of all Mankind. Had I not known this before? I had forgotten. I had forgotten the enigmatic cracks in the fortress of a Hero through which come Everyman and Everywoman. No wonder the Beggar had seemed so loathsome to me when I first saw him in West Street.

3

'The mystery of Space,' said the artist or god in the room. 'Inexhaustible possibilities based on the little that we know.'

I wondered whether he was making fun of me. Seriousness or jollity, it brought home an instinctive telepathy that exists between the sculptor and the sculpted as it runs into evolutions of limited flesh from unconscious ages to now.

'Remember,' he continued, 'that a hundred feet, fifty feet, ten feet may be scaled into a thousand miles. You stand on a map of art which takes you to Shang Mountain in the distant interior. To go there is to dream you know it. How can you know a peak which arose by turbulent if not catastrophic stages from a sea in a valley? An inch may give a million unknown lives or a million insensitive miles. What do we know of the instinctive joys, the instinctive miseries of humankind? We know only our own confusing heroes and villains. We deck them with our own mechanical, popular, parochial values. They become more and more like a machine as they take us into a progressive future.' He stopped for a moment and as his voice echoed in my thought I wondered whether it was he who was speaking or whether it was I.

'Innocent machines,' he said. 'Guilty machines. Not a trace of collective guilt. We have no true, inner, outer antecedents across the ages and we cannot relate to the violence in which they were involved. No reflection in a Bird's wing or an Animal's gait exists in our imaginations to tell us otherwise. We are apart, we are different, we have forgotten to reckon with universalities.' He stopped and I saw a helplessness on his face, a helplessness I felt on mine as well. A curious helplessness. It made me begin, subconsciously perhaps, to drift back into past ages as upon a Sea we were crossing all over again.

'Civilizations come and go. Do they ever return? Can we find ourselves once more glimpsing them as if we have returned? That is a question for the gravity of art. What is gravity? No one can seize it or touch it. It is a manifestation of peculiar attractions that need to be gauged urgently, imaginatively, in art. *Here is Water Street.* Where is it actually? It exists down there by the river and up here on a map of art. A mysterious gravity lifts it and makes it descend deeper than it ever knew. It may vanish for ever as a locality but in its descent its visibility and invisibility bring ecstasy and despair. *Something very frail begins to address us, to plead with us, through Animal or Wing or Serpent we rarely see in human configurations.* They grow by the gravity of art backwards in visionary Time . . .'

'What do you mean by "grow backwards in visionary Time"?' I cried. 'What do you mean by "Animal, Wing, and Serpent"?'

I was at a loss though in some strange way I felt I was beginning to understand.

'You shall see,' he said. 'They are reflections of flight through air, through water, through the Earth we have forgotten. Such reflections tell us of escapes from catastrophes as Earth shook and threw up its peaks. You shall see.'

He paused again for a moment then continued:

'Here is Water Street upon a map of art. Do you sense how old it looks? Far older than the Street below. It acquires the ancient life of frailty when it passes into art. A truly modern sensibility is ancient, is it not, when it is in flight – or potential flight – from a series of crumbling nests. It surrenders to a paradox of Timelessness which is moving perpetually from illusory Time. And it brings a Wing in our bodies that we translate into corridors of Space or into an emaciation where the Wing bulges within and shows nothing but bones that seem to protrude from flesh. *You shall see my quantum pre-Columbian painting.*'

A Darkness began to envelop me as he spoke.

'A scrap of sharpness in a bone in a painted body may point like God's Knife to addictions to cruelty we need to overcome.' He stopped and looked at me closely. I was aware of the ribbed wood of my sculpted body though I had never considered it in this light before.

'Should that scrap disappear,' he said, 'should you – as Bride and Mother of Humanity – see yourself without the Knife of God that takes many forms to remind us of the living Shadows that accumulate around us, then the Earth becomes a blind Battlefield without insight, without conscience. What is insight? What is conscience? *Here is Water Street on the map of art.* It is as important as London or Paris or New York. It has many ghostly and fleshly Immigrants whose flight to South America can only be read backwards in the gravity of Time. You shall see. It is Dark as you drift backwards but you shall see with eyes other than your own. Here is the frail Clock that chimes the passing hours. Look *through* the passage of Time and see how it rolls on the waves into other forms hidden but to be disclosed. Look closely! What do you see?'

I was staggered. What did I see? I looked through the holed eyes of my Mind. Never before had I thought of Mind as a Visionary Eye shared by sculptor and sculpted, painter and painted, writer and written, and extending into many nameless others who create and are created.

What did I see in such a living Void?

I saw a vivid Darkness around me. So vivid it was I felt

myself drifting with Homer's Beggar as he travelled blindly, brilliantly around the world until he came to pre-Columbian South America and arrived – in the gravity of art – much denuded, much later, in a twentieth-century extension of himself, in West Street. He was so different, so disguised, except that he was still a Beggar, that my son did not know him. I – it was – who pointed out who he was. Now my son – whom I created then as a coming god and artist – had re-created me in the Darkness of an ancient world, it seemed, and *I* was blind to certain matters I needed to see. Such is the living Void of art.

The mask of the Beggar was crumbling into ancient fragments one of which lay on the ground at my feet and I was able to read what had been written there by a god it seemed: 'SEATED PRE-COLUMBIAN SAGE WITH A CUP'.

I saw a hole in his forehead, a hole of the Mind, I thought.

'A rounded hole, you may say,' said the artist. 'Do you not see? A rounded hole, a quantum hole.'

I still did not see and continued to read the writing on the fragment: 'He sits like an oriental sage. There's a cup in his right hand. Dice in the cup.'

'Do not tell me,' I cried, 'that he is the Chinese gambler who shot himself. What has suicide to do with the Beggar?'

'You do not see,' said the artist, 'that suicide may spring from sudden remorse, from mental or physical pain that is unbearable, from human resources, indignity and terror, we scarcely understand . . .'

I still did not see this in what appeared in the Darkness of my Mind as a singular fragment and I continued to read: 'His emaciated neck and arms and chest are in contrast to heavy thighs, heavy feet, that tell of millions who have been pinned and slain on the ground.'

'Do you not see,' the artist asked in a voice I could scarcely hear, 'the living Shadow of those millions?'

'I still do not see,' I cried.

'Their frailty is still beyond you.'

He continued after a moment: 'You are so caught in your body as absolute sculpture you cannot see how it runs into paintings backward in Time. It grows or declines backward or backwards in Time into immense frailties we have forgotten to read even in a god's writing on the map of art. There is a community of Imaginations in a living Void created by an Oriental sage *with the Beak of a Bird in the rounded hole of a nose or brow and with Wings in his emaciated chest*. Am I making myself clear?'

I felt his helplessness acutely. He was addressing a world that was so materialistic in me it did not wish to see.

'You write the lines on the Sage,' I cried almost accusingly, 'as if you are a god. I made you into a god in West Street. You were a Boy then. A god's lines are not God's. Who can write God's word?'

He looked at me so helplessly I knew within every Shadow he was still my son. A plural son perhaps who could see a Beak and Wings with rare insight in the configuration of Man. Who is Man? What is Man? I loved him dearly in death and in life. He loved me in every substitute he adopted which took him into foreign lands on a map of art. We were together in a mysterious love that set many problems, many challenges, but triumphed, it seemed, over the Void. Was love, however frail, the essential mystery of art? Was my son's loathing of the Beggar a form of challenging, unusual love that I needed to understand in seeking my Husband?

'It is true,' said the artist, 'that the lines I write on the Sage are partly written by me. Partly mine, I repeat. Others across the centuries have written as well and I have varied my writings, and varied theirs, to make room always for an unfathomable truth. You are the Mother of Space. We are your sons and gods.' He stopped. I had no heart to deny him. I had created him to be my creator. Is the Mother of Space the mother of a Void that reaches into alternate universes of creation and 'de-creation', of Something that dwindles into Nothing we cannot yet explain save that this is the spirit of dialogue in art? Easy to shelve such questions. They touch us too deeply. They bear on the secure and insecure fates of humanity reflected in the passivity of the arts that speak with hushed voices we suppress in ourselves. The artist looked at me as at a live Mirror in himself. In such strange livingness he saw the helplessness he had suppressed. Was the Mother of Space a code of interior consolation? Or did it really live beyond itself, beyond every word he framed? As if in response to all this he continued to speak:

'My writing, as you say, is not God's.' He was looking at me closely. 'I hear your thoughts. I know you. But I cannot frame the true and unknowable God. All writings are from gods who are the sons of the Mother of Space. I know my mother. Do I know my father?' He was staring at me. He touched me, he moved me, once again.

'Who is the Father of Revolution? Tell me. The mothers of all who were slaughtered in the Napoleonic wars grieve for their sons whom they may never see again. France invaded Russia. Two gods not One. The sons of France accumulated themselves into a revolutionary/tyrannical god. The sons of Russia fought under the shadow of a peasant/hierarchical god. Two gods, though they swore they worshipped One. Then again Germany and Russia fought in the two World Wars and Germany invaded Russia in the Second. Russia this time was revolutionary/Leninist/Stalinist/Trotskyite, Germany was exclusive/diabolic/Hitlerite. Several gods not

One. Who is the Father of Revolution? I ask because of Immigrants who have come to South America, ghostly Immigrants, fleshly Immigrants, whom we need to read and understand differently from their individual pretences if we are to appreciate their flight from terror.' He stopped again and looked at me as at the Mother of Space in whom he invested hope for a new vision based on understandings long suppressed in him and in myself.

I pointed vaguely to the woman on my arm (he saw my finger pointing within his Imagination of the gravity of art). I was attempting to say in a gravity-gesture that she was a part of the Mother of Space he was sculpting. Bride of Space. Mother of Space. I looked in the direction of the Sage and wondered whether the cup in his hand could prove a bridal chamber to withstand the dice her husband had thrown . . .

'Who is the Father of Revolution?' I echoed my son's outcry. A line from a poem stole into my mind: ' "Is there anybody in Water Street?" said the Traveller.' Was I not the Traveller? Was Water Street empty or was it full? Had it died in the years that I had passed away or was it newly alive, newly conscious? Had it undergone a miracle of re-creation or was it still a pawn, a conditioned pawn? If the latter, I would have gone beyond it on the map on which I stood. And then suddenly – in that beyondness – I remembered . . . *'Could it be Trotsky? He believes in a permanent, unceasing revolution. You spoke of him as of a god. Unceasing revolution.* Not to be taken literally, but it may be translated to imply the unfinished genesis of all art.'

There was a murmur of voices under the Clock. Dead voices? Living voices? A crowd was gathering there in my holed senses. Two crowds I should say. One stood on the ground of the Street. The other on the map of art close to me. I studied the map with fear and longing. I thought of my

Husband, the artist's father. Could he jump at me out of the map or out of the Street?

Times mingled under the Clock, passing Time, visionary Timeless Time.

This was the year 2000 in a large studio in Water Street. Time was passing, I knew. It was passing through other suicidal Immigrant years in every century. Time awaited the passing of self-inflicted mirrors of visibility imposed like a prison on every newcomer – mirrors nevertheless that could be passing, I hoped, in the unfinished genesis of art into stages of invisible body and Spirit.

Had I spoken my own thoughts now or echoed the artist's, my son's? Without visionary Time fiction is useless, it is but a report on what we already know of the inevitable passage of Time on every Street around the world.

Trotsky had been assassinated sixty years ago in Mexico City, Central America. Had he not passed, since then, into South America? Was his passing shorn of visionary Time? Permanent revolution, however far-fetched, leaves a buzz, like a bee in one's ears, meaningful or meaningless.

Did that bee arouse visionary pre-Columbian figures symbolically assassinated by history in conquistadorial regimes? Did it signify a murmurous revolution in the arts? *Did it signify an organ we need to listen for so deeply, so spatially, so ceaselessly, it fills in some of the gaps perhaps in every fragmented utterance?*

I was prompting my son to make a quantum assessment of Trotsky.

Trotsky may not be *the* Father of Revolution but he could well be *a* spirited symbol of a father passing by ambivalent stages into visionary art. Assassination was one tragic stage, the spiritual husband of the woman on my arm was another, that extended into the Kingdoms of *imaginary* Death (rather than wholly tragic) and a new understanding of Life.

My son appeared to respond to my prompting. He pointed, all at once, to the Bridal Chamber of the cup in the hand of the Sage with the Beak of a Bird on his brow. I had thought at first there were numbered dice in that cup but now I knew better. When I raised my finger I had pushed the woman into the cup. She seemed frail and small. Mother of Space. Bride of Space. Interchangeable numina.

'Do you think China and Russia will father and mother a new world system sixty years or so from now?' I asked my son, the artist. 'For if they do it will require the Oriental Sage from pre-Columbian times to stand at the gates of Death and Life and witness a new *Inferno* and *Purgatorio*. It will require consummate imaginative skill in which all cultures will need to seek their forgotten resources to change and participate. It will require an invisible body and spirit of the Father of Revolution, whoever he may be, who speaks with quantum variations. Such invisibility will bring the shape-shifting Mask of the Beggar into true play. Or else – if none of this happens – it will lead to disasters that will take the world wholly by surprise.'

As I spoke, each die from the cup or Bridal Chamber rolled on the ground or bounced into the air. Each die bore a letter. None possessed dots or a dot to indicate a number. The first die I saw had the letter T on it. The second rolled a little then turned up into the letter R. The third and fourth were lettered O and T. I now read T–R–O–T. This appeared on the heavy limbs of the Sage.

'He cannot run,' I thought, 'but who knows? He may still move a little or trot.'

Three other dice with the letters S–K–Y had fallen on the Sage's chest and brow. A million Shadows seemed to rush up and gain a potential stage of flight never before conceived in this doubling creative way of Man and Bird. They began –

dimly, vaguely perhaps – to perceive themselves within a nest of pollutions, they began to see, as never before, the life of their environments, the land and the water. They felt, vaguely perhaps, the flutter of a Bird in themselves, in the dim backgrounds encompassing them. This was a peculiarly sensitive art that needed to be explored in detail. An instinctive impulse of flight – registered in a flutter of wings – became a measure of distances between land and land, water and water, across which they would fly, again and again, to repair other blind flights they had made in centuries past.

They would fly not only to escape Man-made pollutions but the stresses as well of natural furies and catastrophes. They would fly to enter into a wholly new dimension of which they knew little, to enter into the ceaseless rehabilitation of the living, suffering Earth.

They were held to the ground by the slumbering feet of the Sage but potentially released by his winged body and brow. I could not tell who they were, who their true, shape-shifting, representative spirits were. They passed, dying and living, in the Street under the Clock. They were nebulous but real as all passing populations everywhere are. Passing into Death, into Life? Was Death an absolute? There was flight that left them, ghost and flesh, passing still. I shared with them this ancient, almost-forgotten flutter of wings. An impossible flutter yet wholly possible in the re-creative Imagination.

What a contradiction. It led me into extravagant claims. They were nebulously immortal or timeless, nebulously virtuous, nebulously perfect... Words gave out as they always do and wordlessness brought me to see myself in a sober reflection of the mystery of art.

This was but an inkling of something various and now to be sought, I felt, with a sensation of coming events that could destroy or save. I shared all this with them, I was a piece of sculpture as enigmatic as ghost and flesh. Did I not speak to the artist as he worked in his inmost thoughts on the Kingdoms of Death and Life?

4

My son confessed that he heard his innermost thoughts reflected in my stillness, in what I said to him as he listened to each word that stood on my lips.

Did words stand still on the lips of sculptures or paintings?

If they did one could do no more than wonder at the Silences and the depths of the mystery of language. Sculptures speak. Paintings speak. That was all I could say.

Words have an intuitive formless power as they drop invisibly from the lips of sculptures and bring forgotten parallels into thought, forgotten pigmentations into the faces of characters that are painted in one hue, or changed into another, in the mind of a god or an artist.

I spoke of myself as if I were there and not there, a piece of wooden flesh belonging to a tree I had never seen, a piece of Imagination, imaginary flesh, cloaking the mind's eye with an Animal of Spirit I scarcely knew. Words were a Clock that seemed sensible/insensible on the map of art. They resembled in their insensibility the Clock at the end of the Street even as they differed subtly, profoundly. *The Clock on the map had ceased to strike even as it appeared to echo all clocks*. The Clock at the end of the Street struck loud and clear. So loud, so clear, that it stifled the innermost, open-ended *stillness* of flying Time.

Those stifling sounds were akin to the outer, fractured frame of the artist. What was he, in an outer, explosive frame, that was dying, but a substitute, he knew, a fearful substitute it was, for the Time and Timelessnes of God?

I, for instance, he said, was closer than he to a flight from

Clock to Clock. I spoke with each chime that lingered and broke into the thought of Time. I was fashioned by a hand he knew yet did not fully know, an invisible hand within his biased hand. Bias seemed the appearance of health but it moved him yet to consider the essential illness of art in every unfinished painting in the bloodstream of sculptures.

'I have no doubt about this though I keep it secret in myself. It began when I was a Child – am I still a Child? You are my father and my mother though you claim I have a perfect father. He does not exist.' He spoke in a rash of exasperation. He was human after all though a god. He held his hand as if to remind himself of who or what he was. The hand of an artist surviving in the work it does, in the thought it brings into play in wood or page or marble or stone or canvas.

'You have a father,' I wanted to say, 'and we shall find him sooner or later,' but he pushed me aside as if I were Nothing. He had forgotten his stresses on speaking sculptures. He had reduced me to a piece of Nothingness. Was this not consistent with civilization's eclectic, dead approach to art, to stones that had no value except as stones, no inner quantum life, no inner quantum purpose, to bits of technology that had no value save as dead technology? He looked at his hand and saw it was ill, ill with infinity, not dead. 'I am sorry,' he said, 'so sorry that I pushed you for a moment or so into a museum of Nothingness. Why do I make and destroy?' He looked at me with a kind of terror in his eyes.

He rushed on out of the disease, the material/spiritual disease, that affected his hand.

'It all began when I saw the Beggar and was unable to eat the meal you had prepared for me.'

I looked at him and saw – as I had never seen before – how infinitely ill his hand was. I knew it, his upraised hand, but did I know it at all? It seemed far away from me and yet its intimacy, every scar, every trouble, was in my holed eyes. Was it a modern hand that moved and lived, despite its stillness, and suffered the fires of the ancients? Did it absorb the ailments of long-dead civilizations crying out under stones, under stars, under planets, for new expression? Substitute it was, fearful it was, but it sought the life of creations that bore on the fractured body of Man.

He held his Child-like hand in the air. A Brush with frail bristles with which he painted was tied upon it. The Brush was an extension of flesh. They seemed indelibly joined in my holed senses but there was a Wound. The Wound lay in slight roots, or strings joining a tree I had never seen, to human flesh. Such cross-culturality between living nature and humanity was the timeless instrument of art. A timeless Wound, it seemed, between the appearances of things (one could settle for as a thing) and the Life or the Death of the cosmos . . .

I felt a vitality arising from this wounded hand that edged its way into many cultures. The Wound was there in Knife or Pen as well, glistening darkly as his extended flesh grew into the temptation of absolute violence. Was a Knife, was a Pen alive in inflictions of absolutes? Or were they visible proportions of an invisible hand woven from a variety of substance?

'I knew even as a Child,' he said, 'that I had raised my hand to my mouth – it stood between two mouths in me (I could see them plainly with my mind's eye, one potentially full, one potentially empty) – and it stopped. Why did my hand stop? Did I feel an inner weightlessness that held it up . . .?'

'You loathed your food,' I said simply, 'as you loathed the Beggar you had seen that day in West Street.'

'No,' he cried, 'there was more to it than that. Two mouths

I tell you. I see them now as I never did before. One mouth in Space was old, an old Forest toothed with stumps, weightless in my arm. Why did I say weightless? They – whoever they are – have killed or robbed the Forest of its trees. Yet I see them there still. I see them as I never saw them before. I see the Wound in my hand and arm that make and destroy. How shall I reach the trees that appear to have vanished through me and others like me? An inch on my map of art is ten thousand miles and much more. I see that inch as a quark or something that resembles the symbol of a quark, to put a scientific name of sorts upon it . . .'

He stopped and stared at me as though his eyes and my holed eyes were joined in a Wound of reality. I was stunned by the way he had summed up his art. It was utterly surprising and yet I knew he had followed such a method with quantum variations and with an amazing consistency. I looked around the room at the map of art on which I stood, at the Bridal Chamber, at the sculptures and paintings, at the fires that burnt and yet were an unburning Sea, it seemed to me, to be crossed again and again within modulations of ice and snow or of the fury of Venus and of the Sun. I looked at the miniature elevations of the Street and the Clock, at the Immigrants still pouring in from the drowned *Ulysses* on the crest of a wave.

I looked at the Oriental Sage who stood at the gates of the *Inferno* and the *Purgatorio*. I looked at the gambler's stretched fingers across the floor of the room. They resembled the artist's upraised hand in multiple action, otherness and remorse. They too were miniature Wounds of art changing in unseen ways as I looked at them. I looked at the cave in which the capture of Harbourtown – visualized in quantum sex through the woman on my arm – had played itself to a Van Gogh/Chinese standstill.

I looked at Shang Mountain in the distant Forest.

All were small, compressing tenuous presences and tenuous absences in open, mysterious, unconsuming reality.

Was this the emptiness or other mouth of which he had spoken?

There was much more I saw but I found myself reflecting on an inch as ten thousand miles and much more, perhaps a million.

'What is Timelessness?' I cried.

'Creation throws a ceaseless bridge between Death and Life, between Timelessness and Time,' he said. 'It makes the erasure of something that passes, that appears to be extinguished, into everything with which we wrestle for understanding. That is why I need miniatures to bring into gravity's play what is hidden or appears to be lost or invisible in science and in art.'

There was a hush in the room like the breathlessness of a storm. Was this my own breath resembling breathlessness? It reminded me of the day my son had seen the Beggar in West Street. I felt rather breathless then when I spoke to him. He was destined to be an artist or a god. The thought robbed me of breath. I felt a pang, a nail, as it were, in the painted blood and sculpture he would make of me close on seventy years later. Did I stand then – though I scarcely knew it – on a Bridge between sculpted Death and formless Life? I had never questioned the reality of passing existence so deeply before. If I had, I had forgotten.

Aimless remarks perhaps but they sprang from wooden conventions I knew so well they had become subtly disturbing. They made me feel the breathlessness of things around me with a measure of sudden self-awareness. How deeply self-aware is civilization, in its limitations, about the nature(s) of science? Is it the enigmatic depth of science or is it technology that matches it most closely? Science, I feel, in my thoughts on a plain map of art running nevertheless into invisible Forests, possesses instinctive expectations, beyond one-sided versions of Man, of creations-in-evolutions, evolutions-in-creations, that would set aside the static models and cultures to which it appeared to be committed. It would set aside the very versions Man had endowed science with as though science were a fate. This had been a long quarrel between establishments, or Man-made fixtures, and revisionary discoveries rooted in visibilities and invisibilities. How strange – it seemed to me in my thoughts of sculptured Death and formless Life that mixed enigmatically – that established Man (was he closer to Death than to Life?) and another voyaging aspect of Man (was he closer to a symbol of formless Life?) should quarrel and not be deeply, suddenly aware of lapses in the language they – in their divided personalities – used? Within such lapses it was as though Man dreamt (in an aspect of himself that differed from the establishment of singular Death) of something else that ran disturbingly within his vocabulary and made him unpredictably conscious of relationships he had forgotten between visibility and invisibility.

That was one way of putting myself into a cross-cultural immersion with others – of whom I needed to learn – and with whom I shared a stubborn league that may have been unwitting, with coming or past Death and with a contrary opening beyond fixed lines through lapses that brought the reflections of others into being and broke the tyranny of closure.

It was fitting that I, as the Mother of Space, reposed in strict sculptures of divided Man where Death makes all of one material. *One* material, witting and unwitting, that pushes me back again into several brides and mothers on the Bridge of

Creation. I had shared these with the woman on my arm and there were many others possibly who were still to come.

Bride and Mother point *not* to a culmination of emotions, sexual, mechanical, without love, but to affections so deep they re-open relationships that have been severed again and again within divided cultures, within divided Man and Man...

I felt confused yet liberated by what I had been thinking: *ways of thought that were contrary to a smooth or fixed vocabulary of expression and emotion.* The storm I had sensed in myself was already blowing silent and strong. I faced the artist, my son, on the edge of originality, *his* originality, *my* originality. This was a matter I must probe and contemplate endlessly. It was for me the very essence of living/dead art. Was art one-sided, dominant, singular, on the Bridge of Creation? Or was it plural, plural artist and creations overshadowed by an unfathomable God that gave all gods and substitutes chances for a complex open-ended medium of universality that touched, I would say, a transfiguration that made His unity? Thus it was that I returned again and again to re-opening the Wounds of reality in the arts in which I stood. I had given offence to the artist, who was glaring at me with lightning in his eyes.

'What have you been saying?' he cried. 'You should keep your inmost, *inmost* thoughts a secret...'

'I have challenged you, I know,' I protested. 'I want to do so. I want to challenge the world.' I stopped with the paranoia of sculptured bodies, compressed, agitated, self-created, I felt, yet created by another whom I needed to challenge. 'It's not the first time. It's not the last. Remember, I have been following *your* thoughts. I picked up your remark on "a ceaseless Bridge of Creation. Time and timelessness". Did you say "creation"? It's your thought which I have now expressed in a disturbing way perhaps. Does that make it so difficult? What are words but thresholds into a universal medium of which we know so little?'

The lights of evening were descending and they gave an added glow to the glare in his eyes. I was astonished and yet I knew of such outbursts from the god who was my son. We were engaged in a mortal/immortal play. He was fearful, at times, of all he had done, of going too far beyond the fixtures of a singular tradition. He was prompted to destroy everything he had made in a flash, in a storm.

He continued glaring at me like the lighted Shadow of a man and a vulnerable god in the room. Had I torn a bandage from the Wound of consciousness he carried in himself and was fearful of wholly exposing since it linked him creatively and re-creatively with loathing and with love?

Had I given lights and darkness to what he knew in the unwritten depths of himself and to what everyone knew in the unwritten depths of the Self?

'Never mind what everyone knows,' he cried to himself and to me, 'that is a mystery in tradition...'

'The mystery of art,' I said, interrupting the flow of his meditations within himself and within me, '*the mystery of art* that cries out in every lapse from a programme of belief that is fixed and unchanging...' I considered what I was attempting to say and continued: 'The mystery of hidden relationships between savage gods, secretive gods, savage artists, secretive artists, and the reality they are pledged to explore...'

'Pledged?' he cried in his voice of storm, 'pledged to whom?'

'*Pledged to me.* That's why I am here. You are pledged to me whom you create. You are pledged to objects you assume to be dead, to await inevitable destruction, whatever gloss you put on them, but which are alive in a living, related, complex world you do not understand.'

'What are you saying?' he shouted at me again. 'What are you saying?'

'Not what I am saying. What are *you* thinking secretly, evasively? I follow your thoughts. I am an unkempt sculpture with a tormenting way of expressing what is *apparently* beyond the norms of language. But *you* have taught me this. Unconsciously perhaps. Subconsciously perhaps. *You* have lit a fire, from nature itself, not from fuel, not from matches, but with two sticks or roots or teeth from the Mouth of ancient Space that appears desolated but can spark afresh with a new awareness. Yes, *you* . . .'

I stopped. I could not help laughing at myself, with myself, laughing at him, with him, laughing with stiff, unsmiling lips of Death and Life mingled in a Storm of reality that gripped the room in which I stood. It was a laughter that differed from his even as it resembled his. His lips could move and smile and still conceal his true thoughts which he was fearful of expressing to a blind or a deaf community walking on the Streets. Mine caught the edges of an inner arm within his raised hand. An inner, edged smile which was intent on revealing, not concealing, the stiffness in the walls dividing worlds within and without the Self.

The Storm of Creation broke fully at last, as silently however as it had unobtrusively begun. I sensed there was something unexpected perhaps that the artist, my son, may have been subconsciously planning. If so it would emerge in due course. It would emerge in the light of the Storm in the darkening room. My holed eyes made me see through darkness as through light. The visionary Mind had sharpened my sight. All this, the subconscious waiting, led to his disturbance and to mine. We seemed more adversarial than we had been in the past. But then I knew such adversarial happenings had been brewing in us all along and that they represented, on each occasion, a step forward in the ambivalent relationships of creator and created. I, as mother, had given him birth; he, as a god, had moulded me into what seemed to him an ultimate painting and sculpture.

It was, to say the least, an uncanny, boundless Silence that gave the Storm its preternatural capacity. Was it the faint sounds of distant breezes, so faint they tipped the leaves with the bristle of fluid fire, in ancient Forests? Was it the sound of creation in Shang Mountain? The orchestra played with a fall of leaves building into Time's precarious Earth and Stone from a great volcanic tree.

All these soundless sounds in the Storm of Creation had been lost to art but they returned in a flutter of wings like leaves in a tree. A leaf falls whisperingly and becomes an omen of gravity's wing, it clings to the tree and becomes an omen of gravity's nest.

'Not only Birds,' I cried. 'The nest is also on the ground. It may be seen in a Serpent's coil. The genius of wings extends from air to ground, from flight in the sky to snake-like rivers on the earth along which we may escape from the soundless bite of creation, intermingled with catastrophe, to the Sea that may cloak us with an Animal's skin or sail as we cross from continent to continent.'

There were other sounds issuing from the Storm. I began to hear them now. Was this capacity for a creation, intermingled with catastrophe, the subconscious spring that disturbed my son so deeply he could hardly speak? It had been there all along in his work though its thrust may have seemed dormant. Not only nature's catastrophes but catastrophes administered by a blind and a deaf civilization. I heard distant gunfire falling in the leaves. Guns were falling from the leaves in every Forest. They blasted at Wings and Serpents and at human creatures trying to fly and to sail.

Bombs were falling, as they have been falling across centuries, in the fall of leaves *bringing sensations of a fluid rain of fire* to sensitive and creative ears long before the leaves shaped themselves into blasting bombs.

Maimed children, maimed women, maimed men. I saw them in myself, in my holed body, in a map of art.

I had been sculpted and drawn into a figure of the *Inferno* in which their Shadows dwelt before melting away entirely. *I* had rescued them from absolute extinction.

These were daring thoughts in the poor, sculpted figure of symbolic humanity. They arose, in the first place, in my son. But they filled him with grave misgivings. He was grateful to spill his thoughts into everything he made. Such spilling was a transfer from the god that he was – a transfer of emotional misgivings in the creations he made – into *passive forms of interior Animal Man* who became *active participants* in the making of unstable creations. Man was a substitute for the gods, the gods were a substitute for God. And art – what was art? Art was the *living, psychical* transfer of emotions that gods and men and women felt in their bones. *They moved their emotional bones – intuitively it seemed – into wood and glass and stone and maps and fictions.* Such glass and maps and wood and stone and fiction were an interior Skeleton or an inner Word to be fleshed with paint or to become the blood of holed trees from ancient Forests.

Was it not a form of relief and intimate secrecy, a savage kind of secrecy that he treasured in works of art?

All well and good to see the tradition of the Dantesque *Inferno* as a prison for pre-Columbian, pre-Christian figures but this was a secret of which he could not tell the world for fear of their condemnation. A primal secret of the meaning of creation. Primal secret indeed.

What was freedom? How free was art? Was I alive or was I dead in the prisons of the past?

'You are the Mother of Space,' my son cried accusingly.

'I am,' I agreed. 'You gave me that name and another, the Bride...'

'Yes, I did. I gave you those names, Mother and Bride, as an identity in a game we were playing.' He paused and looked at my frame on the map of art accusingly still but searchingly as if he questioned himself. 'Was it not a game? You were reluctant to accept the names I gave you and I urged you to become involved in the creation of the woman on your arm. Yes, I urged you to become a creator.' He was laughing soundlessly it seemed. 'Do you remember? *All was a game.*' He stopped with savagery, the savage instincts of secrecy and non-freedom in his eyes that I saw in the darkness and the light of the room. 'Did I not tell you – when you asked me – that my feeling for art is so different from popular conceptions that I keep what I do a secret, not for exhibition? I did tell you. But now you are edging away from me. *You exhibit yourself.*'

'I – exhibit myself? How do I do this?'

'I have launched you on the world. *Not on the world.* You confuse me, you make me say things I did not intend or mean.' He stopped and listened to the voices of the Storm. '*In a secret theatre,*' he confessed. 'That was my meaning and intention. That's where I intended to launch you. In a secret theatre. *This* gave me a measure of freedom, let me say, to build and destroy as I wished. To make mothers and brides, heroes and dictators, for that matter, and to break them when I wished.' He stopped again for a moment. 'The world's a secret theatre,' he confided in a voice as low and bitter as the Storm's, 'where what happens, politically, economically, is hidden in its inmost motivations or true intentions for a long time to come when the living are dead and the newly born are indifferent. Art must follow such dictates whatever pretence it makes.' He was staring at me now as though he questioned himself as he had never done before and did not like what he perceived inwardly. It distressed him to speak of such matters. Speech became a labyrinth of unknowns buried deep in himself. The lines of the labyrinth ran on the surface and far beneath in a psyche of terrible meditation I could not easily follow. But I knew how necessary it was to pursue his thoughts.

'Now,' he continued in a flash, '*I know that if I destroy you I destroy myself.*'

I was taken aback by what seemed a flare in a human Storm I shared with him.

'That's new,' he cried. 'It takes me utterly by surprise. Is it all that new? Have we not learnt that civilizations founder when they seek to destroy what they have made or captured? What they *thought* they had made and captured? Such making seems absolute but it is not . . .'

'I still do not know how I exhibit myself?' I succeeded in saying. It was a sombre, still thought that he heard in himself.

'How could I strike you when such a blow strikes at myself?'

How could he strike me when in striking he struck at himself?

Was he helpless? Was I truly alive?

Why ask when I knew I was?

I had known it all along.

But the anguish of his helplessness – the anguish of a god in a Storm – confirmed a transfer of creative powers from within himself into me. That transfer was more far-reaching – in terms of the moving lands and the moving waters and the necessary poise and flight of humanity – than I could perceive. *Poise and flight. Passivity and activity.*

A mysterious transfer of creative powers one would seek to analyse endlessly. And yet it seemed a form of unfathomable simplicity itself. I felt a tremor run through my limbs. I felt a turn in the roles of poise and flight, passivity and activity, I played on the map or theatre of art.

I had sensed flight and activity before in an extension of myself into quantum space. But now the tremor I knew was different. It seemed to suggest an involuntary displacement of myself into another body. That displacement, I felt, would occur from the helplessness of the artist or the god in the room. He would regain nevertheless – in the midst of his helplessness – his game of sovereignty and hold me passive in his hand. Yet it was a stiff hand like a wall between two Mouths. His sovereignty was threatened by the Mouth of Space and the Mouth of Modernity intermingling with pre-Columbian Shadows. A missionary sovereignty, let us say.

I would move, as it were, from activity to passivity and back again by involuntary turns in the play or game we performed. *He* would see me move *beyond* himself. Such was the paradox of involuntary movement he perceived but did not impose . . .

I remembered Dante's Beatrice. Beatrice was two persons, was she not? One sighting was largely ineffectual or passive. The other sighting was different. She did not *will* herself into Paradise. She never knew she had become Dante's guide. And he, the great poet, did not symbolically impose manipulative skills on a *living* divinity. A supreme displacement and transfiguration of one in the other it was.

I – as a holed and poor sculpture of humanity – stood far below Beatrice at the gates of the *Inferno*. Bride and Mother I was but these were substitutes for divinity. Was I an *involun-*

tary self-creation? Did I know one life from another? At least I knew I had to rescue whatever and whomever I could from the unjust prison in which they were hopelessly, it seemed, confined.

The artist glared at me. Then suddenly he cried: '*I tell you I saw you on the Streets yesterday.*'

'Saw me? Impossible. I was here in the studio yesterday. Not me. *Not me.* That is impossible.' I echoed his own misgivings. But he persisted: 'I did see you. Yes, I did. You were dressed as you are now. I saw the holes in your dress. Picturesque and sad. A strange combination of the emotions. I saw your eyes. Black-looking eyes. You were wearing dark, illumined glasses as you are now through which your eyes appeared to glow. Holed-looking eyes. I know them so well. Your hair was covered in a scarf. As it is now. Your skin was anyone's skin. Dark, white, earthen yet like the changing flesh of Sky in the light of the Street. *I saw you distinctly.* I was horrified. You had gone beyond me. And yet I knew that if I struck you – whether you were good or bad – I would strike at something intangible and real in myself. I had created you but I had never considered an intangible, terrifying intimate I released from myself. I could lock you up rather than strike you. But that was no lasting solution. You were there in the Street, I tell you, or in a prison I made and dismantled in my mind. The people flocking around you called you Bride and Mother. An unsavoury Mother you seemed to me, an unsavoury Bride. Yet more real than all the savours of heaven. Your legs looked like polished, fleshy Knives. They reminded me of the creator's Knives I used in the studio. The Street had been beaten down for generations. You opened yourself to every crack. You made it *live* again. But with a life that was terrifying in revealing the illusions of justice and injustice. What is justice? What is injustice? It's a pretence that ignores the wounded nature of the creator. And it piles up apparently extinct – but never absolutely extinct – characters in prisons of the *Inferno* we need to examine and re-examine again and again. Above all when you turned and looked at me I saw your eyes *flash* through the glasses that you wore. I felt a *stab*. A silent stab, a silent Storm. The oddest feeling I should have. Close to Death-in-Life ... Did I need to be rescued by what I myself had created?'

The shock of his words almost made me faint. I felt what he was saying was true. I had been intuitively aware of displacements before he had spoken a word. But now that it had happened I was taken utterly by surprise. I had read his ambivalent thoughts – perhaps dimly, intuitively – even as I asked him to explain what he meant by *exhibition*. South America was a Carnival and a tragic land, it is full of displacements, of people masquerading in a variety of self-creative, wounded ways. How self-creative (with an awareness of the Wound they carried) it is difficult to say. Perhaps it was an involuntary disguise of one in another, the saint in the criminal, the criminal in the saint. I was dimly aware of myself in another. I was rescuer and rescued, it seemed, the rescuer of a god yet I knew myself as awaiting rescue in the universal, complicated arts of creation. I was wounded with such self-knowledge which I gained from the god who was my son in the room. Had he gained it from the Beggar, that Carnival Beggar with his many masks and disguises?

The shock of the moment was so great it left me bewildered and astonished. He too was astonished at the words he had said.

'You saw someone who looked like me,' I blurted out. 'Not me. Perhaps – though you cannot see it – she may know of me, of the sculptures you have made of me, and disguised herself accordingly. It happens in South America, *the Comedy of the* Inferno.' I was laughing stiffly as I spoke, the silent laughter of the Storm which echoed his misgivings and gravest uncertainties.

'Perhaps,' I said, 'you are terribly unsure of the mission you have in mind. So filled with terror at the prospect of releasing the prisoners of closures of tradition and fate – if I may so put it – something that has never been done – that you would wish their lives to remain a game that can never be re-opened or fulfilled . . .'

How had the Comedy of the Inferno *come into being?* The question flung itself at me out of the blue.

A devilishly difficult question. How should I reply?

It had imposed itself upon us – those of us, let me say, who are deemed outsiders, racially inferior or disobedient in charting another faith, heretical or breakers of the law – wittingly, at times, unwittingly, at other times, by closures, a repetition of closures in language and in ideas adopted by politics, economics, and science, exercised therefore by a dominant civilization which sees itself as absolute in its values of communication. Such absolution breeds Death as the final machine or conquistador or creator of things to come. *A restlessness commences amongst gods and artists who seek an openness to all fixtures of language that run contrary to innermost thought, to all closures and tyrannies of convention.*

I had hardly said a word in myself in replying to the question on the Comedy of the *Inferno* when a wordless music arose all of a sudden around me in the Storm of creation. It hit me as it hit the god in the room who seemed unable to say a word. Wordlessness struck my passive lips. His lips seemed passive too: a silent artist or a god in his creation. Not unlike Death he seemed in the shapes around him, bodily shapes that seemed alive. They move or seem to move with lifelikeness. They are unconscious of the rhythms of music that touch other and deeper lives in the prisons of materialism.

He (the artist) had a glimmering perception of this otherness, more than a glimmering, however hidden at the moment. Surely *I* was a part of that glimmering. *I* was alive within and beyond my passivity. With wordless music and the rhythms it brought into being I could rescue those in prison.

Music was a spy I would employ that would reach through all doors of blocked creations.

Music would prompt him to speak to me again – silent and passive as I was – with intimate concern for the life of truth. I was sure of this and of the Bridge or River of Creation he had previously outlined to me in the games he claimed we played. Games, I felt, in which music began to turn his secrecy around into unsuspected viewing by others. Music, I repeated to myself, was the spy that brought new rhythms . . .

I had been warned that nothing was to be taken literally and I had echoed the warning but not understood its meaning in breaking the bonds of one-sided interpretations.

I had seen the emergence of the drowned Ship with its Immigrants into Harbourtown but had not understood the rhythms of the images that sprang from a music in Space that spoke of life within and beyond lifelikeness. I knew all at once – in the heart of art, in its passivity and seeming lifelikeness – that there was a spy of God bringing new-found rhythms into every dead word I had spoken . . .

I had not truly understood – in its rhythmic imageries – the appearance of the pre-Columbian Oriental Sage foreshadowing in his backwards/forwards flight the marriage of Russia and China. Such a prediction was not intended to be taken literally. It was a token of many cultures awakening after a long Sleep to a Dream in the mysteries of Life hinted at by letters signalling a 'Father of Revolution' and the shape of the woman who had been on my arm but was now in her Bridal Chamber.

Had I truly understood my self-creation of the woman on my arm, had I understood the rhythms affecting her first husband from China, had I truly understood Van Gogh's last paintings mirroring a quantum extension of birds, clouds, lands, and the gun that was fired in rhythmic recall of cannon blasting on the High Seas?

All at once the artist found his tongue and spoke to me in the intimate, conversational way one speaks to a sculpture. I had felt this would happen sooner or later. My appearance on the Street had not blocked a dialogue between us. *I was not a thing*. I was a bundle of associations expressive of hallucination and reality. I saw the Roads of the world in which there was conflict or pleasure, in which Man's face was mobile with fierce anger at the loss of his machines and possessions, or mobile with pleasure at the accumulation of new toys and engagements. *I alone seemed to move amongst them with unsmiling laughter on my stiff lips to tell them of the walls of the prison they had built in which were confined their true sensibilities and sensitivities.*

I saw my son, the artist, through my holed eyes and it seemed to me that the map of art on which I stood had become the Street. We were together on the Street. The frames of the windows in the room had become a Skeleton of stiff cloud like my smiling, unsmiling lips. People were passing stained with blood in their strikes for bread or with wine from Carnival.

Pain or pleasure dogged them as they walked.

'Do you know what it is that I hold in my hand?' He had picked up a large Animal Skin from the floor of the room that seemed insentient now under the feet of the passing crowd. And yet without the ground or the street on which they passed they would have fallen into an abyss. 'Let me tell you. It is a Mask of the Beggar on which I have been working for a while.'

The people who passed on the Street descended it seemed from the frames of the Sky or arose from the River and the Sea. They came through the Skin which he had placed on the skeletal windows of the room and which seemed to drape as well the waters and the land.

'I see what looks like bones,' I cried, 'jutting here and there under the Skin, Carnival bones perhaps?'

'Yes,' he agreed and he laughed. His laughter took me by surprise. Was it meaningless laughter? Did it echo the laughter of the Skeleton concealed in every sculpture? Perhaps it did, perhaps it had a slightly different transcendental note in a jutting, laughing bone. The walls of the *Inferno* were as much within him as within me. They may have moved very slightly, with his sudden laughter, beyond pain and pleasure.

'Not only a Sky of bones have we in cloud or mountain or valley but the visionary art of a nose or a lip or an eye or a brow drawn and transfigured from the various poise of the Skeleton we have forgotten as the the paradoxical source of our origins. Curious to put it like that. It gives us, does it not, a different apprehension of populations on the Road. *You* see it, I have no doubt, but it's the first time for me as if I am aroused to the quantum rhythms in the things I have made. It is here in the light of art that employs every line, every protuberance, from the Skeleton we have imprisoned, unconsciously perhaps, without an awareness of its paradoxical, creative powers ... Is it I who have been instilled with the personality of an open-minded god – dim and remote, I must confess, even as it arises within me – or is it they passing on the Street who are unaware of themselves as gods trampling on others in their blind service to conflict and pleasure?'

'Are you suggesting?' I cried as though I spoke from deep

within him, 'that every bone or protuberance from the Skeleton has been enhanced or changed to give an indelible portrait of human character? What is evil then, what is good, springs from an *unawareness* or *a precarious awareness* of the worlds we make, its paradoxes ... I am putting it coarsely as a poor sculpture would ...'

'This amazing work is forgotten but I claim it afresh,' he said. 'It is pre-Columbian but it has a modern feel, I find. The Skeleton on which I place the Beggar's Mask gives me bumps, holes, crevices, from which to make the diverse racial figures of humanity we have imprisoned in our minds *as though they were separate, absolutely separate, entities*. Each bump is different. Some are straight, some are squat, some are narrow, some are full, some make Indian features, some African, some European, some Jewish, some Arabian, some mixtures of these; all may be enhanced, as you said, and subtly changed into a feature from which I hope to look at a long tradition of *unawareness* of models we have neglected that bear acutely on us and on our unity of origins, despite appearances, in them ...'

He stopped rather helplessly, uneasily amongst the people on the map that had become the Street. Had I rescued him abruptly – map into Street – from a frame of secrets he had intended to uphold? It was difficult to say. Was the time truly ripe to bring into the light and dark of time one's innermost convictions? The Chinese Immigrants were there on the Street accompanied by many others from different parts of the world who had fallen through the Skin of the Beggar. They seemed so unaware of themselves, of the world they were making, Time did not seem to matter. It may have been 2000 or 1950 or 1850 or far earlier still. *Time had been killed*. Time had been killed yet it raced ahead on the Clock overhead. Dead Time raced ahead. Were they dead or were they alive? Dead/Living

Time brought a creeping awareness that made them look at me as at the walls of a prison in themselves they saw now for the first time. So it seemed to me in my holed eyes. His eyes, the artist's eyes, were as curiously holed as mine though they were capable of blinking with the passage of the Clock.

I stared at him in his helplessness, in his unease, as though I were guiltily responsible for rescuing him from the dead passage of the Clock in which he played games of art that were meant to be secrets dividing Man into evil gods, into good gods, or into billion-year-old machines without a sensitive depth, a truly sensitive depth, of diverse and living recollection.

'What do you have in mind now with the Mask of the Beggar?' I asked almost apologetically as though I sought a measure of forgiveness from him for throwing a Bridge from the map of art into the Street. Such a Bridge ran like a forgotten river from Sky to Earth. I could see its tendrils through the skeletal frames and panes of the windows in the room. They ran like the varied flesh of the Beggar. They ran across the Sky with an ominous glare that was somewhat alarming.

Did I stand on the Street in such tendrils and flesh? Or on the map of art in the room?

Such questions of living flesh, of inner possibilities to passivity, are acutely relevant to the Imagination of creativity with its quantum rhythms extending everywhere. They are seldom asked, seldom answered by the gods of creation.

His private uncertainties, private questions, had been made suddenly public. I understood much better now what he meant by an exhibition I had staged. Had I been rebellious, a rebellious self-creation, in asserting an independence no one yet understood in the floating nature of consciousness?

Perhaps he was right to feel that the exhibition of private

uncertainties should not come before a ripeness obtained in the Street.

But I felt in myself that the death of Time lay heavy on the world and cried in its heart for a new penetration of universal realities.

Who could say when such a ripeness truly existed and began a precipitation of forgotten tendrils or Rivers or Bridges in quantum extensions of art?

He stared at me in forgetfulness, in fits of exacerbated Memory, for a long spell, and then he said: 'I have fire in mind. I shall seek some model of the origins of fire through the Mask of the Beggar.'

'Fire!' I cried. 'What do you mean by origins of fire?' I felt I spoke his own deep uncertainties that he could no longer conceal.

'Yes, fire.' He stopped in his uncertainty. I felt his eyes in mine. Did he stare through my eyes as though they were psychical telescopes, a Tiresian telescope, blind yet innovatively seeing?

'Yes, fire,' he said again as though he saw something neither of us could properly see. He spoke softly now as if he were afraid of ears he could not fathom in Space:- 'I want the Mask of the Beggar stretched imaginatively far out in Space in your holed eyes – it's absurd, it's impossible, the world will say – to bring someone or something through whom I may *feel* as well as *see* the *life* of fire.'

He stopped again. To *feel* and to *see*, in a creative way, was an impossible task, I knew. And yet I wondered. *Could my holed eyes* really help him? Could they bring the long-dead psyche of the Imagination back to life?

He was speaking softly still but I heard him distinctly.

'We are unable to grow with and beyond fire. Fire is a fury we carry in ourselves, a primal fury, but we have lost the meaning of risk and terror as a necessity for the growth of a living society.' He seemed to be stumbling for instances to prove, or partly prove, what he wanted to say. I understood. I had been stumbling myself, except as a psychical extension of him into passivity and unorthodox movement, I may have rescued him from a pit of secrecy. Perhaps it was impossible to say. It defied literal scrutiny and yet I felt an urgency of consciousness as I floated between the map of art and the Street.

'Electricity is a form of fire, is it not? There are nuclear stations, atom bombs, coal, etc. How long can we keep these going? Are they dead Time racing ahead of us by which we aim to protect our material industries? What terrors do we face, what risks do we need to take, to grow into a truly living society? Are we gambling with Death and Life? Do we know what Life really is?' He was staring at me as if I could provide an answer. 'Most of the saints of the Christian Church suffer, do they not, when we portray their stories, in the hope of glory that they see coming with Death. Life is pointless, it seems, except to suffer and to help others bear their suffering as they wait to die. That is their choice. Ours in secular token is to burn and destroy much more than we need to consume. Do we have an inkling of thought of the pain we bring to the Earth? Our creativity tells us nothing of this. Earth suffers too – I would venture to say – but we cannot *feel* or *see* it as it truly is.' He paused, then continued impulsively: 'Let me give an instance that seems wholly separate but I feel is closely, hiddenly related: the funeral pyre in India. Does it not exist now in South America? A dead man is consumed by fire on a funeral pyre. *With his living wife.* She becomes an object, it seems to me, of the unfeeling Earth. Earth-flesh and human-flesh. Is it that she is wholly passive in the eyes of those who watch her as she burns?'

He was exhausted and silence reigned in the studio for a long while. Days and Nights may have passed for all I knew. I was a diary of Days as Nights, Nights as Days.

A cloud moved over the window-panes of the Sky. It prompted me to speak to him and to let him know that I understood how he felt.

He was staring at a number of pre-Columbian arts he had brought into the room.

'You have come,' I said quietly, 'to the most difficult area of your work. You have been recording what I have said and what you have been saying. And you know now that secrecy is over. The game of art has become deadly serious. Your work belongs to the world. But . . .' I hesitated.

'Yes?' he asked. *'But . . .?'*

'But there are two sorts in the world. There are illiterates, people who cannot read . . .'

'I shall come to those in due course . . .'

'And there are the others, people who can read and write, but who are illiterates of the Imagination. They will dismiss everything you and I say. They will say I am nothing but fantasy. They are materialists. They worship science, it seems, and technological change. But they stick fast to their cultural models. No change there. No quantum extensions there. They stick fast and expect everyone who is weaker or inferior in some way to write and think materially as they do. Illiteracy of the Imagination is the schizophrenia of a language (that does not appear to change) and of science (that appears to change in the new rhythms of quantum discovery).'

He was staring intently, as I spoke, at a pre-Classic, pre-Columbian bowl on which appeared a Child's Face, that took me by such surprise, I virtually forgot what I had been saying.

Would he record what I had said?

Or would it remain in a Void apparently unspoken?

The Child's Face was filled with such terror I was taken utterly by surprise.

I knew the Void. I was part of the Void. Much that I said from time to time vanished into Nothingness. It may not have been heard by the absent-minded creative artist who was unaware of some of his own thoughts. And this proved my independence. I stared at the Child's Face that my son held in his hand. The Void *lived*. Yes, it *lived*. It bore terror and risk in ways beyond the conventional arts. The Void was the Journey of arts and changing literatures within literacies and illiteracies.

At first I swore to myself there was a *blackness* over the bowl on which the Child appeared, a blackness in my holed eyes far out in Space. Was it the blackness of the Void, the terror in the Void? I knew but a part of the Void and could not say. Was it the cloud on the window-panes of the Sky that gave me such an illusion? The Mask of the Beggar had been stretched far out in the Motherhood of Space. I instinctively knew that the Void was immense. So it seemed in my holed eyes.

My son was deeply held by the Child in his hand. It seemed as much to hold him in a tiny glistening hand, in its hand, as he leaned over it. Enigmatic art that seemed curiously to live. There was terror *in* its eyes. Not *of* its eyes. Not made from its eyes. Yet in its eyes like a spider's web of fire and ice. *A thousand years before Christ*. A day in the diary of my sculptured/sculpted book. It had disappeared in the age of blind Conquest – perhaps even before that – but now had swum or sailed to Earth in a Bowl over great distances.

'I shall work with this,' said my son. 'It has popped out of the Skin of the Beggar far out in Space, it seems to me, into the Beggar's hand. The Journey of Life. That's how I see it.'

I wanted to tell him he was speaking imaginatively. *Popped out of the Skin of the Beggar into the Beggar's hand.* It raised enormous immaterial issues that changed the linear language of the arts.

Had Homer's Beggar voyaged to meet the Child, long drowned and forgotten in the Void of Space, or had the Child – in arising from the Void – travelled across galaxies to meet Homer and Plato and Dante and to turn them into partial figures within a psyche of drowned Paradise from which he arose in the hand of shared Imaginations? His hand was Imagination's. The Child's was Imagination's. The Beggar's was Homer's unconscious Imagination's.

'I see the Beggar,' he said, waving shared Imaginations in my holed eyes, 'moving across the Seas of Space until he reaches the galaxies that we know. A small figure he is, as small as the Child's, after an incredible Journey that has apparently worn him down into an eye of Space, a frail star or an eye, let us say. He arrives in the Bowl of a Ship. Is it his Ship or is it the Child's underwater Ship? Or is the Bowl an anticipation of the Cup of the Sage? Bowl and Cup. Ship and Bridal Chamber. Shared Imaginations. He arrives there and sees the Child in the depths. He lifts the Child up into his masked, frail coat. He sees the terror in the Child's Face. Terror, yes. But as he looks deep into the past and ever deeper, he sees Life, the Journey of Life. And he feels *a new brain, a new bloodstream* run through him. An immense cross-culturality – in the midst of terror and risk – he has never experienced before.'

I was staggered and overwhelmed by what he had said.

'Do you see all this in the pre-Columbian Child?' I asked in amazement.

'I perceive the Child as a form of art we have never understood, a form that cries out for shared Imaginations we have never truly contemplated. As I see it looming now my mind races back into spaces unknown, spaces that exist but are unknown. I see those spaces as the other side of Time in the Child's Face. Do you see how double-edged it is? Look at its contrasting lines, its intensities. It is saying two or more things at the same time. As though it knows the weather of psyche in varying ways. It arises, on one level, it seems, from the depths of a Sea of Space and tells of other spaces. It knows, it feels, a multiplicity of universes and speaks in languages we have forgotten . . .'

I sought to transfer what I had just heard into a transfiguration of the map of art, on which I stood, in spatial dimensions. I had raised the map in my holed eyes. He appeared to look through it, seeingly, unseeingly, at the two sides of Time in the mystery of the Child.

'Do you mean,' I asked, presenting his thoughts to him, 'that the galaxy or galaxies which we see, which we now see – which Plato and Dante perceived as perfection or as Paradise – are a watershed against which times run like vast rivers known and unknown . . . ?'

He stared at me, a little aghast it seemed at an Imagination which encompassed much of uncertain scientific detail. 'Put it like that if you wish,' he said at last, half-rebukingly to himself. 'Put it like that. I have no objection. We fumble for words when it comes to creating a universal and diverse myth. We stick to bits and pieces that are useless in terms of deep *feeling*, deep changing. Our institutions seem changeless. The galaxy or the galaxies may be seen as a watershed. Imaginatively speaking. Imagination is my humility. The Child – in this forgotten art, a thousand years before Christ – brings a hint of the other side of Time. The unknown side. We are on *this* side. No, he brings more than a hint.' He was studying closely the lines in the Face of the Child. Did they all belong there or had some been added by another, unknown hand?

'It's there, I tell you. *It's intuitive and counter-intuitive.*' He was moving his fingers along the shape of the Face. 'It's there. To be intuitive and counter-intuitive is to pursue something as dream that we bring to a predictable or a logical end and then to change and find the end we have reached continues unpredictably. There is no end. And *that* is greater than the terror which suffuses the Child's eyes when he arrives on the watershed. He arrives and yet he knows no one can place him absolutely.' He stopped and a thought flashed through his mind.

'Think of yourself,' he said at last, 'arriving as a piece of sculpture in this planetary or solar system. Do you really appreciate how novel you are? It's an original occasion, is it not? You have never been here before in your present attire and shape and innovative being. You are new life in apparently old flesh and wood. You represent my mother but you are different in the flesh you now wear, the *life* in the flesh. I speak of your wood as flesh, animate wood it seems to me. *You are an innovation.* I may call you *Mother* but you are a new work of art. Where do you come from to attain such newness? You hint, let us say, at timeless spaces beyond yourself, *beyond me* who has made you. A paradox. I have no idea how you have sprung from me when I am supposed to have sprung from you. I can claim you are mine but you are touched by an unfathomable God in unfathomable spaces. I have made you, yes, but you are *touched* by an unfathomable Creator on the other side of Time. The map on which you stand is a subtle transfiguration. Myth – in a true however absurd sense – has approached fatherhood and motherhood in this way. Think of Zeus and Pallas Athene. Think of Egyptian gods and goddesses. Think of Christ. Who is his father, who is his mother? The life of the narrative unfolds within yet beyond flesh-and-blood. An answer is there, a partial answer, in a diverse assembly of arts ancient and modern. That is the supreme mystery of creativity that we lose at our peril.' He paused for a moment.

'Let me pick up what I was saying a little earlier. Think of yourself arriving in our planetary or solar system. You are hit by fires of ice that burn holes in your flesh. Venus is ablaze. It leaves deep scars in your sculptured/sculpted skin. Mars is dangerous and has to be scouted with the greatest care. It gives you red and other pigmentations which depend on the light of the atmosphere in the Street, in the Sky, and in my studio. You arrive on Earth and find the furies here as well though so modulated they offer Bridges and Rivers along which you may move and learn in miniature and small ways of your escapes across the spaces you have travelled that now have their map in the life of the Earth that echoes the wordless music of unfathomable being.'

He stopped and looked searchingly at me as though comparing me with the pre-Classic, pre-Columbian Child in his hand.

'The timelessness you bring with you is wounded. I see the Wounds in you vividly, clearly. The intimacy of making. I have put the holes and marks in your skin. I have made you into the Bride of the Beggar in whose Mask are fissures and subtle cavities. *The Wound is a curious, creative possibility of bringing together cultures that are separate into an unseizable wholeness.* This provides a measure of genuine healing in contrasts and diversities. Alas I tend to see you as made wholly by me, as my possession. And, as such, I may frame violence into Conquest as a material end I hope to achieve in the domination of all species. If I strike you, or destroy you, with a bomb or a blow, it is a symptom of ownership that I display.

Even here in this obscure Street, this obscure studio, the tragedy of Conquest is active. Surely it can be seen by all who seek the meaning of art and its perversities. Is this not an issue of terror that saturates Earth-flesh, Human-flesh, in the ritual histories of affairs?'

His fingers were fondling the lips of the Child. He fondled them with care. They were shaped like tiny banks of a river or of a serpent.

'A Serpent-Bridge,' he said at last. 'Exquisitely done. He and his crew, the Child and his crew – the Child is a solitary survivor made by art – came not only on Ships but on Bridges and Rivers that we find here on Earth. Intuitive and counter-intuitive. Who can say – except imaginatively – how life actually journeys through fires and floods?'

5

The Streets of Harbourtown were chock full of people celebrating the strange time of South American Carnival. I went out of my studio into Water Street. I was the artist – alone in crowds, unobtrusive, disregarded – who often walked there. I felt like a ghost now, little known to anyone who plied his trade in the Market under the Clock. Yet my eyes were glued on everyone I passed. We were all ghosts, clad in familiar costumes, on the Streets of Carnival.

It was imperative, I knew, to trace the woman dressed exactly – I repeat *exactly* – as the sculpture I had made and placed on the map of art in my studio.

I had conducted remarkable and peculiar conversations with the sculpture – I had accused her of *exhibiting* herself in the Street – but beneath it all I was terribly uneasy about the passage of events that raised enormous questions.

The sculpture in my studio could not *literally* displace herself or itself into animate Carnival flesh-and-blood.

Who was it then parading the Streets, dressed in familiar attire I had given my sculpture, holes in the cloth of her dress, powder of the right colour on her cheeks, a scarf – such as I had made – on her head, her eyes squeezed into holed apertures as black as the eyes I had sculpted?

She was the right height. She looked exactly right for Carnival, height, legs, shoulders, body, all of the right proportions, as though the sculpture had elongated itself magically in my studio.

Was this ironic familiarity the essence of Carnival?

Carnival had become, in many parts of the world, a dead ritual practice of dancing masks, of jolly appetites, kept under rigid scrutiny by stiff-necked police. But Carnival in South America still succeeded – ironically, subconsciously perhaps – in carrying different atmospheres of planetary cultures in perverse, Timeless displacement. Timelessness had lost innovation and become a security signifying one half of the population in prison to save the rest from crime, the other saved half-tied to a map of place in passive, emotional fixture.

Such subconscious displacement earned a match of one with the other in Carnival. Each prisoner danced, half-man, half-woman, and claimed muster as one in freedom's illusory costume.

Was *displacement* the right word? Displaced persons were a hidden theme of Carnival. Immigrants had arrived, had become pawns in the gamble of Industry, and had never gained a sensation of justice or integrity with regard to their own cultural aspirations. They had arrived, had been imprisoned as chattels, or as gaolers of chattels, in which each gaoler was a superior pawn himself. Exiled consciousness came into play in which exile was a cell, consciousness a wall.

Here was an issue, rarely felt or understood deeply, of the terror of Carnival, a Carnival staged by Immigrants.

I had sculpted and painted Immigrants in my studio but had been unaware of *exiled consciousness* within every work I did. Never been fully aware of castaway consciousness unable to realize the true, inner flight of freedom. Such inner flight not only was an escape from catastrophe but helped in sighting place, wherever it was, as bordering upon – as engaged with – an innovative and living medium. *Without such philosophical and creative vision consciousness remained a familiar form*, a conventional form, to clothe every gun one made in league with a material god, or every aeroplane one mistook for the vessel of God, or every bomb one dropped as the vengeance of heaven. *These forms would strike at their makers. They would be familiar and material dress but worn by strangers. They would strike when least expected in Carnival explosive display.*

Thus it was I perceived that my sculpture of the Mother of Space could turn in exact costumery into subjective parallel with a gun that left holes in the skin of wood, or with an aeroplane or with a bomb.

It was the exactness of copied design – worn deceptively, it seemed, by a stranger – that left me dumbfounded.

How could I own what had been taken so adroitly by another?

How could I know that my ownership of her did not prevent the Mother of Space from becoming dangerous in design, a design that someone else imitated with force and resolution?

How could I know that Mother and Son broke their diverse rules as created and creator when 'mother' became a material code, and nothing else, resembling exactly the intimate sculpture I thought I had made? All quantum variations would be extinguished piece by piece to bring my studio of art to its knees.

Could I save or re-interpret the variations before it was too late?

I was looking now along Water Street, across a crowd of heads, towards my studio. It seemed safe enough but a tremor of anxiety, a faint tremor, possessed me. I felt the sculpture I had made had seized me. *I should have seized it.* No one else around me seemed conscious of this conflict within themselves. The conflict was terrifyingly real. *It was within oneself.* The truth is, I could not tell. Perhaps they were conscious of it in a layer of themselves that divided them from themselves. This division, which they danced in Carnival, brought the conflict to the surface of themselves, sharpened their weaponries and gave them schizophrenic behaviours, sexual and otherwise.

Who was I? Where had I come from to play an artist and a god who judged schizophrenic activities in the dances of Carnival? Had I come from the other side of Time? I had no father but my mother nevertheless had claimed him, in his absence, as perfection. We had never agreed on this. We had quarrelled. We had argued. Was this quarrelling the first, sub-conscious, implicit questioning of myself by an inner, unfathomable Self?

These questions assailed me now, from within myself, so aggressively I felt a split in my acceptance of the sculpture with whom or which I had spoken and recorded our conversations in books in my studio.

It had developed dramatically with the woman who looked so exactly like an imprisoning animation of the sculpture I had made. As though the sculpture were angry and revealed herself in familiar/deceiving terms that made me aware of a one-sided despotic absoluteness I tended to wear as my costume of behaviour at times. So much so she had seized me *now* and not liberated me. She was no longer the sculpted thoughts that had taken on a personality of art and in which I had sensed a focus of Imagination we shared. I had accused her then, where she stood on a map of art in my studio, with my thoughts visible on her, of exhibiting herself in the Street. But I knew even then – despite the settlement we appeared to achieve – that the invocation of the mystery of consciousness, through a work of art I had made, had reached a turning point and climax bringing into action outer, violent activities, that would come to a head in the Street, and inner, terrifying motivations in myself of uncertain unity and escape.

Where had I come from to be an artist and a god who judged and created the world as I did?

I tried to shake off the questions, to resume the admirable settlement I thought I had achieved in books in my studio, but they (those questions) pursued me from within myself like the dances of Carnival, an ironic dancing it was, in my case, pitched from a withinness that made me quake and shudder. The masquerading woman whom I was seeking had vanished for the time being in the crowd of dancers. I would need to seek her again. Not to seize her, as she had seized me, but to confront her and to find a hidden distinction in her that would liberate me. A silent distinction perhaps beyond a gun or a bomb.

I looked around, amongst the dancers, for Lazarus. He seemed, even now, to be peering at me from the Mask of the Beggar. There were several dancing bones and masks. Lazarus had been neglected by European painters and sculptors but invariably, in many South American Carnivals, he was to be seen fleetingly perhaps, unobtrusively perhaps.

Was Lazarus a sculpture made by Christ?

What a question to be asked by an inner Self . . .

It is asked, I feel, because Lazarus arose from his grave like a work of art which is silent, which speaks not a word. Not a word. Sculptures do not speak. Lazarus's appearance, two thousand years ago, happened at the edge of language, an unknown universe of language, when a pre-Columbian sculptor fashioned the Oriental Sage with a wing on his head and a cup in his hand. Humanity believes it possesses a language capable of depicting everything it measures or thinks. But there are edges beyond the fixity of watersheds, edges that seek new concepts in description and design, new variations, and Lazarus arose from his grave into a Silence that cupped a star dawdling a little, far out in space. So he danced in Carnival fleetingly with a star on his head and vanished again.

He uttered not a word. Silence. Silence. A Silence that seemed to blast civilizations falling into their graves as he arose from his. Vestiges of resemblance may be detected in pre-Columbian arts. A fleeting resemblance. Breaking from the surfaces and participating in the depths of Carnival. Nothing familiar from so fleeting a dancer. An *original* resemblance. A blend perhaps, a sharing of Imaginations, of and between the Oriental Sage, at the time of Christ, and the pre-Classic Child, a thousand years before Christ. An original resemblance – I would aim for, as a new, uncertain sculptor – one hand carrying a cup with a brain, a new brain, born of the marriage of civilizations, ancient and modern, the other carrying a bowl swimming with furies far out in Space. The Journey of Life through the grave of Death could only be glimpsed in miniatures in the Silences at the edge of the universe.

Silences, yes, are the true voice of original sculptures. Perhaps I had subconsciously understood this with a wordless music that gave subtle rhythms to the words spoken by the unspeaking works of art in my studio.

Was I a Stone, I wondered, in the Carnival dances? A Stone with the colours of a Snake and the fleece of an Animal. Fleeced stars or wings. Quetzalcoatl. *Coatl* (the snake). *Quetzal* (the bird). Lazarus Quetzalcoatl. Another original resemblance.

The Stone of the dance pulled my feet into an abyss that carried the brain of a star and the bloodstream of a river.

The River beside Harbourtown was about to turn. It had indeed turned but could not be easily detected in its turning as it descended gently to the Ocean.

I bent my ear to the River. My ear seemed a particle of fine substance in and above the slow-flowing body of the River.

I had arisen from the grave of the dance, from its material combinations. The doors of such combinations needed the shock of the furies to unlock the *Inferno* at the edge of the universe where brain and bloodstream were to be glimpsed in the Silences of Space.

Thus it was – here on planet Earth – the Stone I danced had turned – despite an abyss – into a flowing, life-giving stream.

I was above yet within the bloodstream of Space. I was within all modulations of fire and of every known and unknown element. They offered me terrifying glimpses of the Journey of Life through hells and infernos and furies. I was filled now with hope and despair. Hope existed but despair remained that every weakness for material superficial aggrandizements would prevail.

I listened at the Stone – which was a configuration I felt to be my Carnival self, inner and outer selves – and I heard the distant, ever-approaching feet of armies marching to conquer the face of the Earth. I placed a trembling cloth of water over the Skeleton of the Beggar in myself and in the depths of Carnival. This brought me into fearful juxtaposition with past recorded events danced by bands opposed to one another. Were these bands within me, without me, a withinness, a withoutness?

In the midst of the fever and the savage turmoil of the dances I kept my eyes glued to my studio a little further along in the Street. It became an important tossed-up miniature of civilizations, a peculiar, massed, material house yet a psychically broken Library of the arts. I saw its window panes reflecting the Sky and the Earth like broken halves of the Stone I was. A most peculiar feeling. Nothing was settled without a visionary language to re-interpret the ruined fixities of recorded history that baffled gaolers and prisoners alike and kept them divided and in place. I saw the walls of the studio floating in the River, blown to bits by a party of dancers, blown into sliced bones of the Skeleton I had seen there in the River. I knew this was the vision of a Dream but it could actually happen as it had indeed happened in recorded histories. The dances could erupt into violence as had been the case before. They had not done so as yet today in Carnival but it could happen in a moment of fever and unconsciousness.

And all at once the pieces became keys. Crucial keys I needed but had with difficulty understood, keys to unlock the masses of absolute aggrandizement I feared. Keys that were coming into my visionary hand held aloft on the Street too late, it seemed, to serve their psychical purpose.

'No,' I cried, making an effort to understand afresh my visionary hand which was itself a key, 'No,' I cried again – 'it is never too late.'

The Library at Alexandria was danced in a Stone between an abyss of violence and a faint-flowing River. Had they not seen the Stone becoming a star and a life-giving stream? They had not, I said to myself, and was chastened by such condemnation that was a plague on myself as well as on them. How long had it taken me to see Stone, Abyss, and River as a living potentiality and not as the *Inferno* I had been blindly conditioned to behold? The Library was now consumed by imaginary, dancing fires. I saw the blaze on the Stone of the River, reflected lights held in flaring bowls. The fires were happening in Alexandria. The Arabs (in a body of Carnival dancers and marching feet) were invading Egypt. Centuries ago were written today on a trembling cloth of water.

I could see it all as though my studio and the Library in Water Street, South America, were threatened. The mass of the Library at Alexandria had grown, generation after generation, into a prison of unwitting materials, imprisoned books and other lifeless materials, they seemed, since Alexander the Great had imposed his will on the known world. Now an unknown re-interpretation, unknown to him and the establishments of the world, secreted itself in keys no one understood though they danced and marched on the edge of understanding.

The keys were scattered pieces and miniatures on the cloth of the River. They should have been nurtured and perceived, created, re-created, as visions of change, slowly, even painfully, again and again, but they lay now in fiery disarray too late to avoid a furious catastrophe.

The Library at Alexandria had housed Jewish, Arab and Hellenistic cultures, housed them in its prison but brought no deepening cross-culturality between the Jew and others. The dire estrangements remained to torment history like a changeless motif.

So did the Carnival dancers in Water Street now imply. I looked through them, with them, through their subconscious/unconscious eyes that littered it seemed – a litter of gazes or estranged letters of performance – in Stone and River: a withinness/withoutness in the dances I half-dreamt I was involved in as I kept my eyes glued to my Library and studio that seemed intact and as yet untouched. They would not touch it today I felt.

I wondered whether the *unburning fires* I had lit within had saved it. Such unburning fires cultivated keys I may not have realized were there. They kept them in a state awaiting creative use . . . It was a random thought perhaps but it gave me some encouragement in the miracle of visionary art.

What did my Library and studio house with unburning fires that lit the window-panes like a distant Sky, lit the floor and the boards and the ceiling? It housed, I felt, a protective and inviting array of books and arts. I had reached the studio now and as I entered there was a riotous flow of dancers beside me in the room. Shadowy reflections on the wall and the floor. They were partly transformed or translated by the fires that burned and still did not burn. Yet I feared they might still take something with them that was precious, that seemed an end in itself to me, from amongst the works of art in the studio and the Library. It was a riotous flow indeed. They swarmed over the pages of my books which I kept open on a table and a shelf. Their entry into my studio was possessed of the small feet I had heard in the Stone. A denuded army they seemed as they raced into and out again of the cave at the end of the room. Denuded but still threatening as they grouped themselves in fires and outside of fires. Outside their Shadows grew as large as ever. I saw them, small and bunched on the fingers of the hand I had painted on the floor. A shining street each finger seemed on which they swarmed. I watched the River from the window. It seemed to flow within the house. Each cloth of water recorded tiny lines and psychical adventures, denuded adventures that brought sudden ruin to every place they touched. Such was the mystery of the dance. Each page in my Library was a cloth that trembled . . .

They swarmed everywhere on Brides and Mothers of Space. They were lines and Shadows. They swarmed on the pages of my books, in the Bowl of the Child, in the Cup of the Sage. They ransacked the letters that declared 'Father of Revolution'. They seemed to stop for a moment at the sculpture on the map of art. I heard them whisper as loud as a Storm in the Silence of the room: a sound like torn paper, the sound of pages on which I had written my conversations with the Mother of Space. It was an ominous sound that ran into music I had not suspected. It brought me a clue of the dancer I had been following earlier in the Street. She had concealed herself and disappeared in the tumult of Carnival. Her familiar dress had seized me before she vanished as a god who claimed to have made her, subjugated and manipulated her to his own ends. I was that god but I could not believe it. I found myself dumbfounded by the sculpture on the map of art – so passive she seemed – and the costumed dancer, resembling her so closely, active on the Street.

I turned to her. She was my sculpted Mother. 'It's not you,' I cried. 'It's someone else who has copied everything so closely she has grown by unburning fires into *you*. It has happened here with the dancers. They have become as small as you but sometimes they recruit their own Shadows and grow large . . .'

I waited for her to reply. But she was silent. The dancers had now gone as swiftly as they had arrived. The room was vacant. The cloth of water on the River that seemed to run through the room had ceased to tremble.

'Speak and tell me,' I cried again. 'It's not you and yet . . .'

I looked closely at my Mother.

I prodded her. I beseeched her. I asked her to say a word. But she was silent, her lips still and incalculably beyond the shape of my thoughts. I could not make her speak because I wanted her to do so. It had always been a spontaneous eruption within me and within her when I addressed her. My thoughts appeared spontaneously on her lips and in her eyes that I had fashioned as if it were not I who had made them. Though I often insisted it was I. Had I not made her?

I had not made the quake of the Earth within the living wood fragmenting into burnt branches and indestructible seeds when the volcano comes. I had not made the rumbling awful silence of the lava that is modulated still to bring the spirit of consciousness we rarely understand.

'Something has happened to me.' I spoke softly in great sorrow. I spoke to her in her Silence. 'I have returned to a door in the past I never understood though I made it, or seemed to make it, in the vibrancy of youthful energy and fire. I raised my hand and made it invisible at the table in West Street where I was unable to eat. It was a Day of sorrow and preparation. I was a Child then. It was a Day that all human beings have in their lives, subtly, inexpressibly, but they soon forget. It has come back into my memory by this terrible event. For I see now that the door I made is shut. You have died in your voice and passed through. Another door opens, another opportunity rears its inexpressible/expressible place. It tells me of the father I have never known whom you have promised to find.'

I stopped again and blamed the dancers.

'The dancers have taken your voice. They have stolen your voice. They have reduced me into a Skeleton Child with a Key such as I dreamt I saw in the Beggar's Mask. A Key to open all doors. One is apparently shut. The other is apparently open. Are there other doors of which I know not?'

6

Despite a measure of damage, and torn paper on the floor, I was fortunate enough to save my studio and Library of arts from destruction by the invading dancers of Carnival. They had entered like a band apparently ready to make headlines in the News. This was a deception and it gave me room to translate them into unfinished figures of Time. They stole voices and papers for purposes that went too deep for reportage or casual understanding. I had clothed them in armies, ghost armies that were terribly real nevertheless of the living past.

This was a phenomenon for the year 2000. How could an artist revisit his innermost Selves in others he had treated as non-existent or as unimportant and create defences against ultimate catastrophe?

There are indestructible seeds in the Earth when the fire rages. Each seed grows into another country in the language of art. I was – to say the least – in two places at the same time. I was a revolutionary player, small as a seed perhaps in the News, while maintaining myself as a rootless, intractable Stalwart of everyday events. As such I could participate imaginatively in public affairs, in their hidden depth, range, reality.

Riot and theft are public affairs in the News. My sculptured Mother of Space on her map may have understood this with irony when her voice was stolen. Her Silence was a profound irony. It was a shocking theft I myself would have to wrestle with to understand, an inner Self wrestling with an outer shell of being that offered varieties of room for understanding.

The inner countries of the mind come into their own with bursts of Memory and Imagination, unexpected, unpredictable, that may steal what one prizes as one's absolute possession.

I may need to see myself in others as large and threatening in an inner country of the mind, I may need to descend into a Skeleton Child scaling walls and prisons he has himself made.

As a Stalwart of the News I am inclined to be uncertain of every entry into an inner country I make and so I read the printed tale of Riot in the News like a half-Man, a half-Child in my uncertainty.

This gives me some congruence with the wooden Mother of Space who has lost her voice. Have I lost mine? Am I as silent as she, whatever verbal noise I make, in the language of the News? Do I have visionary room for anything else beyond the word of the News?

WATER STREET LIBRARY RIOT. BOOKS STOLEN AND DISMANTLED.

Such dead accuracy in the News is a closed door. What passes through is finished and imprisoned for ever. It is an end in itself. It is a source of sorrow. Celebration – whatever that means coming with or after sorrow – may only arise in inner countries of the mind. Can one's house, one's village, one's city, become an inner country . . . ?

The answer lies on the floor of the studio.

This is the clue of which I was told when wordless music touched the dance of Carnival.

I take my Key, which it is said opens all doors, and unlock the riot of papers.

With these curious pieces, it may be possible to build afresh, in a more knowing way, that begins to account for all the edges, the Library of arts in which I stand. A universal Library.

At last I have unlocked the paper or clue I seek. It is a letter shaped in its crumpled state like a fragment of battered door. I place it on a table and smooth its lines to apparent perfection.

It seems unimportant at first as I read it again. It is an old letter. Yet it writes itself anew, it becomes a living edge in my hand as I reread it. It tells me, in an odd eruptive way, something I had known for years and discarded as finished, something that returns now with a curious, unfinished urgency. It tells me I had sold the house in West Street where my mother had lived until her death in 1952.

I had put it in the care of an agent in Harbourtown. He had written to say the sale had been arranged. A woman would buy it. He would bring her to my studio in Water Street. I would have to sign certain documents. The studio seemed new as I reread the letter. The Key in my hand had unlocked the vacant room as if Time had drifted back to an inner Day I had discarded as an everyday business event. Now it was returning afresh. I am tempted to paint the shell of Time as it returns with uncertainty as absolute African or absolute Asian or absolute European pigments but these absolutes dissolve into partial Semitic and pre-Columbian brushstrokes. Lazarus Quetzalcoatl hovers in a vivid atmosphere in my Brush in the studio. Lazarus arises from his grave and brings past Time into life again. He becomes for me a nameless atmosphere though I may call him Lazarus within the shell of Time. He is as nameless as I, as representative of other civilizations which I grope to know. The past is genuinely aroused through such cross-cultural atmospheres in art. It returns. It ignites an inner pigmentation in the mystery of Quetzalcoatl, in the colours of a Snake and a Bird . . .

Thus it was that the agent and the woman have returned in my studio and are as real as if they had come today.

The agent busied himself. He is in the past. He prepares the documents I am to sign. He is in the present.

I am aware of the woman in my studio as if I had never seen her before, neither in the past nor in the present.

Was she a dancer yesterday in Carnival? Had she hidden herself? Am I blind to appearances – though I seem to know them well – or am I to an inner being within appearances?

Who am I? Who is she? It is an old question that returns in a new way and it compels me to focus on the reality of identity I dreamt I possessed. I do not possess it. It possesses me.

I paint her as a fine-looking woman dressed in a trouser suit that fits her to perfection. She is the right height for the dancer in Carnival who had hidden herself. She has stripped away the robes of the sculpture she may have worn. Her face is free of powder.

I do not know her and yet I follow her present/past gaze with a curious, inner knowledge, the intensity of her eyes as she looks at the sculpture whose voice she has stolen as before she may have worn its entire aspect as her disguise.

It is the strangest blend of today and of a well-nigh forgotten yesterday in an abyss of Imagination in which I have dipped to paint.

I hesitated for a long while and looked across the vacant room. I saw her standing before me in a painting, as I hoped to paint her, and outside of the painting. She was in and out of the painting, she was real – in and out of immediately graspable flesh-and-blood that challenges the eye – and I spoke to her with an Imagination that sought a blend of opposites, interior and exterior. Without a blend of opposites, however painful, however apparently desolating, humanity would deceive itself for ever in its laws, customs, rituals, and exactitudes of Time. It came like a timeless flash as I spoke sharply, awkwardly: 'I am sorry. The sculpture of the Mother of Space which fascinates you is not for sale.'

I listened for her reply. Would it come? Yes, it came from her two-angled, inner/outer presence, across Time, within Time.

'I like her and her attire very much,' she said. 'There's a woman now in prison. Drugs is her crime. She has been sentenced. I shall dance for her in Carnival. You shall see me and then lose me. But now I am here. I am a Thief and an Angel who comes out of the past into the present to stab at all complacency. Do you believe me?' She had turned and was staring at me where I stood dumbfounded. 'There is something in the sculpture of the Mother of Space, as you call her, that reminds me of the prisoner. Something pre-Columbian.'

She saw my astonishment and walked across the room to a shelf of books. 'Here it is,' she said. She had opened a book entitled *Before Cortez and Pizarro*. The numinous picture at which she pointed was of *A reclining woman, 600 bc, Ancient Mexico*.

I was taken aback. 'The Mother of Space reminds you of this?' Once again I found myself looking at a piece of sculpture and at what stood outside it, or within it, in a public, apparently inscrutable domain, in a vacancy of language, that came to life across two thousand six hundred years.

'She certainly does. She reminds me as well of the woman in prison. Remember that. There's the scarf on her head around a new brain we have never understood. Universal consciousness. And the eyes! Holed eyes. They sleep and are awake. Ah! yes, they sleep and are awake in the music of the stars at the edge of Time. Are we, are we still sleeping? Do we know where we are in our parochial, everyday business in which we miss the mystery of returning Life? Mushroom eyes, hallucinogenic eyes, black stars. We lock her in the prison of ourselves. We lock her in, who brings the farthest Sky. Is this what prisons are for?'

I remembered my hoped-for painting. I remembered the blood of the Mother of Space I had dreamt I had seen. Could I blend them into their opposites? They spoke silently of my father whom I now glimmeringly perceived.

Here was a work of art that staggered me in its *in-ness* and its *outness*, its *blindness* and its *seeingness*. I saw magistrates, judges, politicians in my vacant room. None was my father. I could not see him. They were in and out of the painted canvas I had in mind. I heard their articulate logic, the sentences they passed. They did not question who they were, where they came from to exercise such absolute authority. The prisoners they condemned were equally conditioned and confused. I listened to the Angel's word all over again. She had indeed spoken like an unfinished Angel. Angels, it is said, converse with humanity. How do they speak? In a disjunctive voice they steal from works of art. Thus they make themselves partially understood and bring together shocking opposites we have taken for granted as eternally separate.

Vacancy is the lifeblood of Timelessness.

What do I mean by *vacancy*?

I mean the subtle, apparently unimportant happenings – to which one pays little attention – at a business engagement. I had sold the property in West Street – it had once been my home – years ago. That was a business matter. I had not seen the house that I had sold over all the years that had passed. I had been obsessed with the game of art in my studio in Water Street. But then the woman to whom I sold the West Street house had returned suddenly, through a letter on the floor of my studio, in the vitality of numinous Memory. She loomed when she came with all the subtle, unimportant details she possessed when I first met her. These now grew into a realm of opposites in the vacancy of my room.

I saw her as flesh-and-blood in the vacant room. Flesh and blood are very important but they become a shell in the architecture of Time. I sought to paint her but her flesh-and-blood became a door requiring a Key I possessed but did not know how to use on this particular occasion: a door to an inner pigmentation I could not properly grasp though it seemed more real than the real.

My life had changed when the sculpted Mother of Space, on a map of art in my studio, had seemed to project and exhibit herself as flesh-and-blood in the Street. I had followed her in Carnival – doubting my own reason – but she had vanished amongst the turbulent dancers. And now I saw that she was here in the studio, that the woman who had cleverly disguised herself in the robes of my sculpture, was none other than the one who had returned from the past into the present dressed in details that strengthened into a suit. And yet she remained an intangible challenge, the ground of opposites, the past and the present. Her voice was more than my voice, more than the one she had stolen from the Mother of Space. It was rhythmic, disjunctive, conjunctive; it filled me with a numinous terror.

The vacancy of my room became the ground of opposites, sorrow and celebration, times past and times present, interiorization and exteriorization, ruin and origin, absolute, cruel authority and the creative/re-creative fulfilment of an endless Love beyond material images of love.

'What do you mean when you speak of "more real than the real"?'

The question stung my Imagination. There were spatters of rain that painted the window-panes of the room with small drops and architectures of mist. The voice I had heard had come from the glass of history. 'More real than the real' was painted on glass – the glass of a window-pane, in this instance – to tell of the terrors of global warming humanity ignores. 'More real than the real' may sound absurd, may look absurd, to the ears and the eyes of normal people.

I considered the question.

'Normality is rife with complacency,' I replied. 'The atrocities perpetrated on Native Americans were dismissed as though they never occurred: atrocities perhaps worse than the Holocaust. Four hundred treaties were signed with Native Americans. All were broken. Business reasons, land grabbing, etc. Yet subtle, apparently unimportant pressures remained on the glass of history like small drops of architectural blood. The Rain was a Timeless signal an artist such as myself could not ignore. Natives who complained of a broken treaty were put in prison. Some scholars and anthropologists estimate that seven to eighteen million Natives were alive when Columbus touched the continent in 1492. I speak now of North America. The figures for Central and South America are as terrible and alarming after Cortez and Pizarro completed their Conquests. As far as the Natives of North America go, we know that in 1924 fewer than a quarter of a million – out of seven to eighteen million – remained. Their ancestors had been slaughtered, victimized, starved, across the centuries, vacant centuries that carry the life-blood of Timelessness.'

I stopped and gave further consideration to a question that moved me profoundly. Would I ever paint the glass of history?

'It isn't easy,' I confessed, 'for one to see how conditioned one is by intellectual mechanisms that sustain the logic of one's age. Intellect first surrenders to a mechanistic logic, born of a conditioned mind, in which it prides itself as being supremely objective and natural. This is an illusion. It has happened with the Cinema. Native Americans have been portrayed in the Cinema as savages to be manipulated, at best, or gunned down before they committed their worst, cinematic horrors. Cinema became good, best-seller business and it conditioned the history of centuries into materialistic and intellectualistic aggression. The practices of slavery and exploitation, exercised by imperial powers, did not affect the arts in a profoundly cross-cultural way. In fact, they were drawn into painting parochial and dominating pigmentations for characters of which no evidence existed of true colour and shape of features. Environments, lands, rivers, were felt to be dead objects that could be used by human agencies... Thus it was I stumbled, in my game of art, into wood and paint and glass as factors in a sacred life that projected itself – against my will it seemed – into tangible/intangible flesh-and-blood. A revolution in sensibility requires a knowledge, transcending intellect, into vacancies, if one is to overcome complacent politics, complacent law, complacent morality...'

I was aware all at once of the prisoners in gaol I was being told to rescue. There was the *reclining woman*, charged and sentenced to five years for drugs. There was Lazarus. He had been sentenced to seven years' imprisonment. He was called a dangerous trespasser. He had come out of a trench in which he slept. It was a grave to which he belonged. He had brought unwelcome news of a past – that no one desired to contemplate – into the present.

There was the Sage, a middle-aged man, wretched-looking in his body, as though wings were sprouting there, who had stolen a cup from a wine-shop. He claimed it was his. It belonged to him ages ago, he said. He needed it now as a gift for his daughter who was to marry a Russian anthropologist exploring Harbourtown and out into the Forest as far as Shang Mountain.

There was a Child-like man who stole a boat and was sentenced to six years in prison. He swore it threatened to sink but floated like a miracle-coffin. Was it a coffin? I reflected on Herman Melville's *Moby Dick*. The *Pequod* sank from the Sky of Space to the bottom of the Ocean. Queequeg's device, labelled a coffin, may have sprung from resources in cross-cultural legend of which we know nothing. I saw the Child-like man's craft as a Bowl in an imaginary painting.

There was the Beggar, an illegal Immigrant, it was said, of whose crime I was uncertain. He had been imprisoned for ten years.

A grumble arose from the Street. Was it the mysterious voice of the Beggar? It was the sound of a machine passing in the Street. The Carnival dancers had gone. And yet their presence flitted in a butterfly's wing on the window-panes of my room. The glass was broken slightly in places. An eye, on a wing, no larger than a delicate area of subtle green and blue and white and black, settled for a moment to spy and copy the exact costumery of the sculpture on a map of art in my studio. This had happened when Carnival was in preparation. And now I saw again clearly, more clearly than I had seen before, the mystery of preparation which I might easily have brushed aside or forgotten.

I looked across my room – from the butterfly's human eye that danced on a window-pane – towards a painting of the Beggar. He seemed to be speaking to me now as softly, despite the sound of the machine on the Street, as the butterfly's wing. Had he seen the woman when she returned again and again to my studio and made secret notes of the robes my sculpture wore?

His place, though here, confined in my studio, was every-where. Even in stolid, apparently lifeless machinery, his voice could be heard, accompanying the butterfly's wing, in the mechanical business of everyday events.

He was an illegal Immigrant. No one knew where he came from. He brought spaces with him, in the painting, that ran in tendrils or ribbons or fragments in the leaves of trees, shaped like wings, ran through man-made cities and uttered a sound in soundlessness.

He could not be defeated by man-made machinery. To place that soundlessness within a grumbling sound was beyond my Imagination, beyond all human limited Imagination.

The sound of a grumbling voice came from a passing machine but in combination with script and painting it seemed to issue from a butterfly's delicate lines in a human head. Or was it an Angel's eye peering in with silent music into my studio? Such music could be stirred perhaps by genius on a piano or an organ or a violin or a flute as a Brush seeks to stir tangible flesh-and-blood from intangible, unfathomable creations.

I was persuaded by the Beggar to visit my former home in West Street. Little though I knew it, this was to prove my first self-portrait. I had painted nothing of myself before. I had kept myself in the background, fearing perhaps to give a fixed pigmentation where there should only be inner colour in the architecture of Time.

I arrived in West Street unprepared – despite all the work I had done – for what I saw of the makings of an unwelcome self-portrait. I was greeted by the greatest shock I have ever had in my life. *My former home, in which I and my mother had lived, had disappeared and in its place were the white walls of a prison.* The garden with the waving sunflower had gone. A trifle perhaps but profoundly meaningful to me. It was a diary of years of life I had sought to conceive afresh, to capture freely afresh . . . I had failed perhaps I saw now with the bitter promise of a self-portrait I had never visualized before... I noted evasive particulars around me with great numbness and shock.

The authorities in Harbourtown had approached the woman to whom I had sold the house and the land and had bought them from her. Why had she said nothing of this to me? I had come to see her as an Angel and she had apparently practised a complex deception upon me. It seemed deliberate. Was it spiritual terrorism? Or was it a dialogue with the Unknown? She had squeezed me into a clod of earth on the road. An unshapely clod, it seemed, which I kicked into the gate of the prison. Was it myself that I kicked? I and It felt nothing at all. No mental pain at first. No psychical lesions or cuts in the flesh of earth I had trodden for years and felt little or nothing of its deep-seated kinship to me. I had worked with the furies of the Earth – as a god and an artist – but had remained religiously, philosophically, trapped in their numb mysteries.

But now slowly, by degrees, numbness became a true source of terror.

Numbness arose.

Was this my self-portrait?

Windows were tinctured into eyes, modernistic eyes in a white-walled, primitive painting. Barred ribs. Terror continued to grow. I felt lost, squeezed, broken.

Who, if I cried, would hear me among the angelic
orders? And even if one of them suddenly
  pressed me against her heart, should I fade in the strength
    of her
stronger existence? Is beauty nothing
but beginning of terror we're still just able to bear?

I had put 'her' where Rainer Maria Rilke had 'his' – *her* heart, *her* stronger existence.

Terror, the terror of Angels, persisted. But I was still 'just able to bear' the unwelcome, hideous lineaments (they seemed) of a self-portrait which featured the prison where my home had formerly stood.

I felt as though I had died and had returned to find a world so different it took my second breath away. I was a Nobody in the world around me. Everything had changed. And yet I remembered wooden, Child-like, Nobody fingers – that may have been a reflection of mine – uplifted into a raised hand at the top of the prison. 'No,' I said to myself, 'a wooden, lifeless hand could not be mine. Wooden, lifeless hands belong elsewhere, in other parts of the world I do not know. There is a division I do not feel between hunger elsewhere and the food I eat. An unfeeling division. How does it reach me, how does it make me feel my unfeelingness, save through an Angel of art I fear who brings terror?'

I felt for the Key in my pocket and wondered if I could mentally project it into my raised Nobody hand at the top of the world. The guard at the gate instantly came forward and I told him my mission was to help and console the prisoners within. He opened the gate. He took me to another guard, who led me along a corridor to the prisoner I desired to see.

His boot was flaked with lumps of mud and he inadvertently shook one of these into the cell. It lay there, curled and reclining, beside the woman in the cell. I reached out through the bars and picked it up. The place where we were was wholly different, it seemed, from the table at which my mother and I had sat and had our meals. And yet I remembered the moment when I had come in after seeing the Beggar and been unable to eat. Was it the barred window close to the cell through which I looked into Space? I saw only the sky and the leaves of a tree. It could have been anywhere in the world.

The woman had risen and approached the bars of the cell. *She was pregnant.* This was a surprise. In another month I reckoned she would give birth. This held me in the midst of my terror. Was my self-portrait the prison, the mental prison, in which she was confined? Had I helped to build it with a lifeless hand? The thought of walls of architectural Time flashed through my mind. An impossible thought, a terror-stricken thought, but it seemed utterly real. Humanity in me surrenders itself, year after year, century after century, a blind surrender, in which it does not see the *Inferno* it is building. It surrenders its deepest sensibilities, its deepest insights, to wholly material satisfactions. But a Key of art remains, as I knew, to unlock terror through variable Angels.

I turned to the woman at the bars of the cell and spoke beyond the ears of the guard. 'How can I save you, how can I rescue you,' I said softly, 'when you are so far gone with child?'

She stared at me with her black, holed eyes that were glimmering now. A black star is a deceptive eye in Space whose light shines faintly, darkly. She said nothing but I thought I read what she was thinking in the faint but strangely powerful reflection in her eyes.

'*I* shall rescue *you*. Not you me.'

I was staggered.

'*You* rescue *me*? What on Earth do you mean?'

She stared at me from a great distance, it seemed. *Far from Earth, it seemed. Godless, distant, intimate eyes were staring at me.* I was stunned by an apparition such as I had never seen before. And yet it was intimate. I knew it. Had I not seen it, even made it before, and not known what I was making?

'Do you not believe in a god or in God?' I spoke impulsively.

She listened but said not a word.

There was neither belief nor disbelief in her eyes. They were more mysterious, I suddenly felt, more deeply mysterious than Godlessness or Godliness. They were at the edge of the inexpressible . . . I tried to get her to speak but could not. 'Is *that* your view?' I cried. I was helpless. God and *Godlessness* were man-made terms in her eyes I saw now for the first time. One may project them to the edge of universes. One may feel one has taken them there. Perhaps such a projection is necessary – in this world, this man-made world – to achieve a reconciliation of opposites, a transfiguration of God and Godlessness, that brings us closer to the inexpressible truth. One may take one's partial language to the edge of moving origins. But when one tries to fix it there as an Absolute it becomes a fatal illusion. It threatens, then, music and art and science.

These thoughts – if thoughts they were, they seemed so unaccountable, so unpredictable – flashed through my mind and left me more helpless than ever.

'Do you feel,' I cried, 'that music and art and science will become nothing but shells we parade for entertainment, profit and technology?'

There was no reply but I saw her reclining, one arm held out as though she were assisting an invisible personality, representative of many who were threatened.

The guard came forward. He walked realistically like a person going about his everyday duties. I, on the other hand, was conscious of hideous self-portraiture; I remembered myself projecting the Key of art into the walls of the building as if to create a mirror of possibilities; I saw the guard now with a mud sculpture on his boot, which he did not perceive, and which he inadvertently pushed into the cell; I saw the top of his head looming up in the world like a president's or a prime minister's. No mirror was his in the walls of Time. It was a dazing, unwelcome vision for me, mirror and all, but I knew that without it nothing would ever deeply, truly change whatever appearance of change it might have.

'I am sorry, sir,' he said, 'but I see you have had no replies from the prisoner. I do not know what you were saying. I was a little way off. Remember! she is drug-addicted. She is being treated but her mind wanders, it seems to me.'

'When is she expected to give birth to her baby?'

'We shall send her to the prison hospital in a week or two.'

He spoke mechanically. He and I, I sensed, were farther apart, though he did not know it, than the reclining woman and myself. She and I had gained an intimate relationship across the great distances – that seem small as a stone or a pinprick in the Sky – dividing man from man. A miraculous relationship. Such miracles were possible but they required unpredictable voyages beyond static traditions, an unpredictability – save in furies of violence – that was lacking, it seemed, in dominant cultures.

Dominance tended to impose itself on everyone in a universal cell of language. But the distances remain, I knew beyond a shadow of doubt, beneath mechanisms of universality, unseen perhaps, unrecognized perhaps. I had glimmeringly sensed a rhythm that spoke of Bridges through the eyes and gestures of an estranged prisoner, partial Bridges that were miraculous and disturbing.

I left the prison in a state of turmoil.

A mirroring prison that turns stone and wood into remorseful art – which one sees however glimmeringly in past and present abstract dimensions – may turn as well into an uneasy vista to revolutionize civilizations.

All languages, however apparently alive, are cells of a blind gaoler or guard or politician or citizen of state who believes they are immortal even when the soil of discourse disintegrates under his feet and tells him he is an unconscious artist carrying on his boot flaked sculptures of his prisoners.

Latin is a cell on which many a boot still claims to rule the world. The reclining woman had intimated to me her miserable subjection to many cells, many biases, many prejudices, that hemmed her in and made her declare for a speaking Silence. She was closer to the edges of universes, with their words imbued by partial and ceaselessly inadequate assumptions of the meaning of Time, than one realized. This was her ancient humility.

She had intimated to me that the walls of Time had sealed and locked her away within the biases of ruling cultures and made no mirroring attempt to go deeper than the skin and vessels she appeared to wear. Nevertheless I had talked with her through those obdurate walls. It seemed impossible but it was true. How had I done this? What revolutionary art had I stumbled upon to bring her into intimacy despite the normality of the *Inferno* and the great, hidden distances that stood between us?

I returned to the studio with my imaginary self-portrait in mind, intending to start painting soon. But first I placed the mud sculpture of the reclining woman beside that of the Mother of Space. Even here – in an unconscious piece of art – there was a curious resemblance to the carefully plotted work I had done of the Mother of Space. It struck me all at once that such resemblances – like an accumulation of variable insights I had gained from my own work – were obscure but they told of a human forge of traditions in all creations – how else could I now put it? – which drew the blood of earth, mud, stone, wood to run into the flesh of Imagination. Perhaps the Angel had brought me a sharper and more bitterly probing or extensive eye than ever when she opened the book *Before Cortez and Pizarro*.

I remembered the guard's insistence on an addiction to drugs that made her mind wander. She was a twentieth-century woman, and nothing else, in his eyes, that differed from mine, who needed to be hemmed in by the law for her own safety. Drugs were dangerous, he felt. This was true. But his eyes were conditioned by a single aspect of things that enlarged them into a block to sensitive truth. Flesh was a block. Wood was a block. There was no kinship. It was impossible for him to link her to the stars. He had no idea where she came from, who she was, where she was going. He called her 'the silent one'.

He pictured her as single-faced, one-dimensional, and this gave him the illusion of an exactitude of drugs in a wandering mind.

The Picassos of his age might dabble in many-angled, many-faced portraits born of African pieces of art lying neglected in a Paris marketplace. Picasso's intuition of an African, shadowy past informing the one-dimensional status of photogenic European women would seem to him utterly incongruous and absurd.

My perception of a pre-Columbian diminutive presence informing a twentieth-century prisoner would seem a Nobody abstraction to him.

Nobody. Homer's Odyssean Beggar had escaped Polyphemus, the Cyclops, by stating his name was *Nobody*. Did the blindness of the Cyclops signify a condition that bore on the present day? Was the guard in the prison, which had been my home, a blind (however clear-sighted he seemed) Cyclopean, modern gaoler? She (the reclining woman) had said she would rescue me. Was I a prisoner groping to understand who I was, where I had come from?

These thoughts straddled and tickled my mind into laughter intermingled with terror.

I opened *Before Cortez and Pizarro* and saw a series of diminutive or figurine sculptures of the reclining woman.

The first to strike my eye lay on the ground. Her body – above her thighs and beneath her breasts – was like a balloon. A pregnant woman. Resembling the prisoner in her cell. Her holed, black eyes were the same. But the round balloon she carried indicated as never before a mathematical alteration to her body and limbs. It looked like a bowl or a cup turned on the outside. It seemed ready to move into the air and to float away.

Bowl or cup. I recalled the Oriental Sage with his Cup and the pre-Classic Child on a Bowl.

Frail and small assets, but they spoke to one another through nebulous image rather than adamant word. Were they closer to the language of the stars than the cells of modern words?

Did they (those assets) speak of the moving origins of the universe, a dawdling, shaking Ship, a Bridal Chamber, far out in Space, yet here on Earth?

Had I come from such a seed or art of the womb figured in the stars?

Was the womb a Ship, or a Bridal Chamber, in quantum variations?

I was born, it seemed, of a movement of the Self beyond the Self in light and darkness: figurine sensibilities I could not capture. The inner radiance was too intense. No blocked largeness but a seed through which we grow in wisdom, decline into apparent Nothingness, and escape the Cyclopean guard of the *Inferno*.

My first haven, so to speak, or transport to Earth, was a mirror of possibilities, a Bowl, a Cup, a Bridal Chamber, a Ship. I came as a seed from one world into another. And my shape now, my human shape, seemed fixed in the world into which

I had arrived. It had been fixed for ages, it seemed, body, limbs, head, eyes. It had been fixed but it carried a mathematic of flight into great distances.

What is Timelessness? Is Timelessness more a sensation of travelling Spirit than of fixed Body? I put aside for the moment the book with the series of the reclining woman. I seized a canvas and placed it on a wall of my studio. It was time to start painting my self-portrait. The shadows of leaves came on the canvas in my studio like the brush of an invisible painter and gave me a clear, terrified view of the walls of the prison that had been my home before a change had happened to its garden and its rooms. *Now* it was the body of a prison. Could I recover traces of the spirituality of home?

I stood at the gate of the prison once again as I had stood when I came upon it unexpectedly before my visit to the reclining woman. I stood there once again with the memory of the sunflower of childhood like a cup or a bowl on my head. A trace of the spirituality of home.

The bars in the walls of the prison were about me. I brought the Key of art from my pocket and opened the gate. I was imprisoned before I had properly entered except that the sunflower brightened the prospect. It was a constellation that I painted. The seed, the Bowl, the Cup, had grown and opened itself into a stable fire on Earth. It isn't easy – I knew from long experience – to paint fire. Fire rages and burns but needs to become the body of a flower one cherishes. One forgets the borderlines between Body and Spirit. To fail to remember these is to condition oneself into a loss of origins in a universe of furies. Fury becomes an absolute. Each body is an illusory eternity and there is no modulation of the furies. One imprisons a body and does not see where it comes from. One loses all compassion and inflicts violence upon it. This Cyclopean blindness rules the world as it did in Homer's age.

Once inside the prison I was taken by the Cyclopean guard to a cell in which I was placed. He did not know me. He appeared to see me but his one-eyed stare was so accustomed to occasional bars of sun like paintings in the corridor, to the leaves of trees that were taken for granted casting their shadows through a window, that there was a failure to interpret spiritual/material limbs, such as mine, erupting from the architecture of Time.

It was an eruption that played with the skeleton Sun and the veined leaves, an eruption – as in a play of creation – that made them into diverse or wholly separate-seeming creatures, the flesh of a god or an artist or a murderer or a thief.

He saw them, the veined leaves and the skeleton Sun, as a fixed shape in the cell in which he had put me. I was fixed. He remained blind to the balloon of Spirit on which intangible I and tangible they had come and on which the Beggar had lain long ago in Homer's age. A ram-shaped balloon or a hill laced with the hidden fleece of unpredictable Rain or Snow or Sun. *Nobody* was there. I was there.

Nobody and *Faceless* were cousins. *Faceless* stood in the corridor outside my cell. I saw him there, as I emerged from my cell, amongst a group of prisoners. He came over to me where I stood by myself. *He was Lazarus.* His face had not been properly painted and I could not help noting how nondescript it was, apart from what seemed blazing eyes, so nondescript it seemed *Faceless*. He turned to me and spoke, much to my astonishment.

'I am still to rise from the prison,' he said, 'therefore I can speak. Immediately after each arising I am silent for a while. I shall arise soon with Quetzalcoatl. He will return. The world will be driven on his return to nurture the species it has murdered, the birds, the snakes, the fish, the whales, the seals, the lambs, the sheep, the tigers, the butterflies...' He listed an interminable series of destroyed or threatened species on what seemed the facelessness of the Earth.

'Is the Earth *faceless*?' I cried.

'It is faceless to a humanity that sees nothing but what justifies its inordinate lusts and pleasures. Everything is the same. The small veins on a flower's wing are not seen as eyes on a window-pane. The tiniest creature is crushed by a boot as the whale is speared by a harpoon. No one sees any difference except the strength of violence to be used. I arise, time and time again, to make the different universes on Earth live afresh. Their unity is in parallel complex formations that we need to care about creatively and re-creatively. I have no absolute moment when I arise – when my coming out of the grave is finished for ever. I arise again and again. And now I shall arise with the new coming of Quetzalcoatl – *quetzal*, the bird, *coatl*, the snake – for the species Man has murdered without a thought or a quiver of true guilt.'

I was utterly taken aback by what Lazarus had said. I became silent and unable to speak. Lazarus Quetzalcoatl stared at me with his blazing eyes from a faceless mask, it seemed.

'You may call me *Faceless*,' he said. '*You* have become like a sculpture and silent as you thought I would be. Such is the fate of Time, it displaces itself into freedom, freedom into fate. In such displacements and subtle transfigurations you may look for me when I arise from the grave. I make men into passive sculptures of psyche but I turn passivity around into unsuspected, inner life to an order of things we take for granted. Such turning is a miracle no one understands. They take it all for granted. And thus they are subject to terror, the terror of outraged lust and psyche. Violence may have its roots – who can tell? – in outraged lust and psyche. You see now, do you not, how the Mother of Space puzzled you, distressed you, when you saw her walking on the Street. You had made her yourself as a god and an artist but you found it virtually impossible to cross the borderline between a game of privacy and a living, truly active publicity. She arose, as I shall facelessly arise, in a moment no one understands, though we are all involved in it. Was she familiar, in wearing a costume you knew exactly, or was she a complex deception, as faceless as I am now, that plagues you into seeing your art differently? Such subtle differences between familiarity and complex deception, in the arts we practise, may make for resurrections of psyche that obey a principle of destruction and violence to compensate a universe that starts afresh. There is a clash of ages in a moment that we do not understand. When I say 'obey a principle of violence' I do not mean this literally. The language that we use is a cell and it is inadequate. But I trust you see how all-pervasive Lazarus is. I am the hoped-for edge in all meditations, in all self-portraits. I disappear and I reappear. I am subject to weaknesses born of living a life again and again through others that see me as faceless in their material, familiar pastimes. I await now for a call that will summon me out of this prison.'

There was a Silence throughout the corridor. We may have been standing at this or another edge of a painted universe. It was a dazzling, confusing edge of Silence. There was a cloudy Rain-filled Sun and a shaking leaf. The corridor stretched into traceries of home. I saw a window in the Sky that I remembered, a clump of wood and a tree as though I looked back from the future into the past or forwards from the past into the future. It was a confusing vista of presents-in-pasts-in-futures awaiting alternative arts of understanding. I saw the Cyclopean guard with his blind eyes painted in myself and others. I shed his skin and adopted another portrait of myself through which I saw more clearly. A blend of the skeleton Sun and a leaf shook in the mysterious cloak of Rain. The Rain was falling heavily, it seemed, and providing a cloak for Lazarus. There was a commotion within the corridor. Two men appeared carrying a stretcher on which lay the reclining woman. They were taking her to hospital a mile or two away in Harbourtown.

My voice was suddenly, inexplicably restored. I spoke. I said: 'Lazarus Quetzalcoatl, the rain is your cloak. It falls with music. Take this and let it beat overhead like a subtle, ballooning drum. It is an umbrella. You must hold it over the woman on the stretcher. Some may see you but the majority will dismiss you as a myth or as an hallucination. The Shadow of the Rain on a tree. Enter the ambulance outside. When you reach the hospital you are free.'

The guard stood at the bars of my cell with an impossibly innocent expression. He barked at me: 'The prisoner called Lazarus has escaped. An ugly bastard. We shall catch him sooner or later. We shall catch him, I promise you.'

I said nothing. The words I had previously uttered had sprung from me involuntarily, I felt, as if compelled by imaginary freedom so long suppressed they seemed the words of fate. Who was Lazarus? I suddenly wondered. Was he a rebellious atmosphere a painter might encounter in an artifice of walls? Did he contain others in himself? Was he a Man or a Myth a painter might seek to paint? I had called him *Faceless*, a cousin to Homer's *Nobody*. I remembered his blazing eyes and the incredible things he had said. I was glad he had made his way out of the prison. He seemed both nebulously and strongly alive to me. He seemed to be the answer to a long-sought question I could not now define.

The guard was staring at the walls of my cell as though he hoped to find Lazarus there in a mingling of imaginary fates and freedoms long suppressed by the duties he performed. He suddenly barked afresh like a dog on a chain: 'We have given you permission to paint and to draw on canvases on the walls of your cell. You said you were making a remorseful self-portrait. We are interested in confessions of guilt. Is *this* your self-portrait?' He was pointing to numerous drawings on the canvases on my wall.

I felt as if I were confronted by someone who wished to buy a painting of mine in my studio. He was drawn to them and yet reluctant to admit his fascination. He seemed Cyclopean with a one-eyed stare and yet impossibly innocent.

I attempted to explain: 'It is a peculiar, large-scale portrait of myself which is linked to others on psychical horizons, it is also a portrait of a Man in the bars and the walls of a prison that are parts of himself. You see the bones through the flesh. Inner bars. Inner/outer walls as well. Old ruined buildings of ruined civilizations carry the fragmented shapes of horses and riders, warriors, hunters, saints, priests, made by dense and persistent atmospheres of Rain and Sun and Storm and Mist. You will find yourself there though I have never seen you as innocent as you now look.'

He seemed surprised by what I had said. Was he on the wall of the cell? He did not see himself there. He saw himself as someone seeking to buy a work he wished to keep under lock and key. A prison is a prison is a prison... For him a prison is everywhere. It is a bank, it is an investment, it is profit, it is cannibalism. Perhaps a painting would fetch a good price in time to come. A painting was a slave, a living slave.

'Innocence! *I* am innocent. *You* are guilty. That is why you are here in prison.'

He stopped – utterly convinced despite his meditations on prison – and stared at me closely. The bars of my cell stroked my face. They gave me a white appearance as though the paint I used had spilt a little on my skin. I could not help laughing through the paint and this disgruntled him yet his innocent expression remained. Had I painted him as innocent without realizing what I was doing? A wall is a wall is a wall until it bears wished-for, longed-for traceries of home, a cosmic and an impersonal/personal tracery of home. The innocence of a Cyclopean guard is a tracery of wished-for, longed-for protection one had hoped for in an eternity one called home. This was an irony in the life of paintings, a life beyond one's calculations of finished line, finished shape, closure, contour. My home had now become a prison. And this came as a great shock to me when I visited West Street. So much so it lit and extended the seed of Imagination I knew in the womb of Space, in the multiple Bride of Space. *I returned to my studio but found myself borne back afresh to West Street in a self-portrait that raised me above myself and linked me to others within cycles of familiar/unfamiliar psyche which are the natures of art.* Within such cycles a room is a room is a room until the weather of Space and Imagination breaks it back into longed-for traceries of home. Home becomes an obsession. An obsessional prison? An obsessional studio?

Everything is now more real, more terrifying, more open nevertheless to new possibilities, than one thought it was. The life of a painting, the innocence of canvas or wood or stone, becomes an astonishment that makes one see the Spirit of the Mind watching the body's passivity. Paul Gauguin had painted a woman lying passive on a bed with the spirit of the dead watching her. The mind is alive, not dead, and it brings us into deceptions between place and place, between the watching dead and the watching mind, that animate reality into vital considerations of who we are, where we go, where we have come from.

'Have you heard of Oscar Wilde's *Dorian Gray*?' I asked the Cyclopean, innocent guard. 'Wilde was imprisoned a century and five years ago.' I could not tell whether his reply was affirmative or negative.

'*Dorian Gray* tells the story of a young man, impeccably handsome and presumably innocent. He has a picture of himself which is a true likeness and which is stored away. He commits deeds that are debauched but he retains his youthful good looks. No change occurs in him. *Only the hidden picture ages and acquires the scars of debaucheries.* No doubt Wilde sees this as a witty fantasy but it impresses me as the intuitive life of art. A consciousness beyond individual fixtures of innocence exists. Consciousness is a mystery. Mind moves within and above all and sees, ages, knows the innermost deeds that are hidden from the passive, automatically active body. The picture is a profound version of mind that lives and offers a field of inner, complex action beyond ourselves, within ourselves, that we rarely explore. We lose our ancient, diverse ancestry and deceive ourselves with static descent that seems determined by fate. The far-reaching, moving deceptions between the Spirit of Life and the Spirit of the Dead become inactive and therefore are unable to bring us out of provincial miseries into unpredictable discoveries that embrace strangeness. What do we really know of ourselves? We write still in fixed nineteenth/eighteenth-century forms into which we pour twentieth-century experiences that remain unlived in their relationships with the past. We are confined in a cell of language. We imprison ourselves without understanding how or why we are imprisoned. The furies descend. Our civilization tightens into a threatened place. The Spirit of the Dead watches our sexual adventures. That seems the best we can achieve. We may hide this in frills and opportunistic dances that seem cheerful but such cheer is a vanity.'

There was a clamour from the corridor of the prison. It was like the sound of nails being driven into the walls of each cell, into the walls of flesh. My cell tightened upon me. But yet I felt I understood something new of the prison of a civilization, of an artifice of walls that seem permanent. I had investigated this before but it had remained without the sanction of a god. Now it began to acquire a deeper relationship between the past and the present. 'She's dead,' a voice cried. 'She's dead.'

'Who's dead?' I thought I knew but I still asked.

The guard swung away from the bars of my cell. He moved into the clamour of nails and voices as if he were venturing into Space. 'The drugs woman is dead. The Silent one. She died in hospital . . .'

'What about her new-born child?'

'The child's alive. The child is strong.'

There was a Silence now descending everywhere. We stood at the edges of starred, nailed Space, it seemed, in the corridor of the prison. So it seemed to me. And I remembered the constellation of Lazarus and Quetzalcoatl whose promise had come true. A Man is a Myth. *A Man and a constellation bear some part in opening up the tapestry of a living, partial language into meanings that have been imprisoned for ages.* Such imprisonments are fixed. But at last they move subtly in their cells, they move beyond themselves. *Lazarus, in my paintings, was a moving part of ancient Quetzalcoatl and he promised, in such movement, the emergence of a new Quetzalcoatl.* Who was Quetzalcoatl? Samuel Beckett's *Waiting For Godot* had been first appreciated in a prison. So I had been told. The nail in the flesh helps us to see an inner, far-reaching, mixed creativity between technology and the music of genesis that one never dreams one possesses.

Quetzalcoatl had been utterly amazed when he looked into the Smoking Mirror and saw he had a human face. He was the god I had been waiting for. Beckett may not have found his Godot but I had. A failed god I knew, but he gave me insight into Spirit and Body, into the artifice of walled flesh. He had felt his spiritual life so entirely that he patrolled the world doing good for those who needed him. He helped his sister. He helped kings and their subjects. He was wise. He was compassionate. He saw the faces of men as poor, drugged creatures, obstinate, fixed, unable to exercise their imaginations beyond a series of crippling fact. *When he realized he had a face like theirs – when he stumbled upon it in a Mirror – it came as a blow to his senses.*

He lost sight of the good and the great things he had done. He accepted the narrow accounts, in the rumours of people, that he had seduced his sister. He took on himself a responsibility for crimes he had never committed. He was staggered into a creed in which the image of Man is the image of God. And yet he clung, perhaps forlornly, to an unfathomable Creator in whom a Spiritual art, beyond fixtures, mirrors the promise of Man however desolate that promise may seem.

Was this not a new beginning – frail and ancient, perhaps, but immensely significant – that civilization today has never considered creatively or understood re-creatively?

I wrote this question on the wall of my Harbourtown prison. Harbourtown is an obscure land, few have heard of it, it is South American, it is a small corner of world civilization; but such corners are foci and in them may play long-neglected beginnings that have no place at the centre or centres of world civilization.

Quetzalcoatl – a long-neglected god – had seen himself as Man in a Mirror and had learnt of the deceptions a god may play on himself. Yet – through such deceptions – he began painfully to sponsor an art such as I had intuitively and counter-intuitively immersed myself in, with quantum variations that have no end and no beginning.

I was often lost, filled with terror; I had gone under Seas on a window-pane in my studio, been subject to ice ages in drops that freeze and fall like skeleton tears from the Sky, but found an imaginary footing, beyond myself, once again. 'Beyond myself' brought me back into home and prison, into unsuspected revelations of myself in others and with others.

The sins that Quetzalcoatl took on himself, in my paintings and sculptures, lay far beyond fantasies of debaucheries. They were the sins, of which a civilization is ignorant, of a failed, universal Imagination. Such a failure indicates the suppression of different cultures – the loss of parts that differ even as they point to a ceaseless, unpredictable whole – a suppression by ruling, material dominations, within an array of facts made into absolutes by fixtures of language that possess an inferior and conquistadorial place to benign Spirit, in human affairs, on which Quetzalcoatl had prided himself. There are no absolutes he learnt with pain and with suffering. One needed to probe, to revise, to see oneself from different levels of which Spiritual and Imaginative art was one.

Am I not deeply saddened by the death of the reclining woman who had been accused of an addiction to drugs? Yes, I am. It is a moment of loss in which I struggle to regain imaginary steps into the meaning of drugs. Perhaps that is why I wrestle with conceptions of Quetzalcoatl whom she is said to have brought back as a Child. Yet Quetzalcoatl has no beginning nor end. His birth or rebirth is an abstraction that tests us to the core, an ancient core, a modern core. In ancient times, when he stumbled on his Face, he had implied that the 'the faces of men were a revelation to him of poor, drugged creatures'. He saw 'drugs' as 'addictions': addictions to power, to money-making scandals, to patterns of lust, addictions unseen, unknown, stemming from a haze that rises between Man and reality. This haze makes Man blind to shared innocence and guilt. I felt I must look closely at the apparition of the reclining woman who had passed me on a stretcher in the corridor of the prison on her way to hospital ... Yet once again I was immersed in the new and the old Quetzalcoatl to whom – I had been promised – she would give birth. An abstract and a varied birth. Would this provide an explanation of drugs beyond factuality? I found myself immersed in – as I said before – or caught deeply by a sculpture that I kept hidden in my studio. *Hidden in a room like the cell of my imaginary prison.* Quetzalcoatl burst from this like a Dream. He towered aloft, seated in a chair, on a plinth. There were six or seven companions, all seated, behind him, the last of whom was a woman. I was struck – though I had made the sculpture – by the appearance of the men behind him. They wore round masks on their faces like a slice from the Cup of the Oriental Sage or the top of the Bowl of the pre-Classic Child.

Zero-like masks.

Zero, I now remembered, had been first invented by pre-Columbian cultures and had become a mathematical marriage between East and West, North and South, where figurations and calculations of Space were now made.

Zero exercised a peculiar pull on Quetzalcoatl who had arranged his new-found features to express layers and levels. He looked like a Figure passing from one level into another. He looked from 0 into 1 into 2 into 3 into 4 ...

I was struck by the holed, black eyes of the Mother of Space on her map of art in my studio. She looked through Cup and Bowl. She had died, her voice had been taken away, something in me had died, giving birth to Imaginations more varied than I dreamt I was capable of.

Yes, she had died and yet here she lived afresh in the Figure of Zero that gives birth to Quetzalcoatl. It was a symbolic birth. It could not be taken literally. Quetzalcoatl was ancient and modern. He was an abstraction, intuitive and counter-intuitive. I have said all this before but it comes back with subtle and new force and changing power in my mind.

Her holed, black eyes had become zeros which adorned the faces, or the facelessness, of Quetzalcoatl's companions. Lazarus had implied that Man is Myth. And, as such, Man becomes a powerful, unconscious agency, in quantum figurations, to revolutionize the world. Man has not awakened to his invaluable role as Myth. Until he does he is blind to other levels of himself and is doomed to think he has captured mystery in machine.

The prison hospital stood on ground called Lost Paradise. An unlikely name for any part of Harbourtown. It was a name that defied an ordinary understanding. *Loss* signified something that had once been there but had failed to remain or had vanished. No one knew what had been lost since no one entered into far-flung, intimate discoveries of what had been previously there. They saw mechanized grasses, mechanical bushes within a haze and assumed everything had always been like that. They could not sense that they had directly or indirectly sliced the world and made it as it now was. Such slicing was a form of art, unconscious as it was, and it required a new and ever-unfinished dialogue of great sadness or remorse or even joy with a living, subtly living world that suffered and could be turned into a net of horror. Joy was a reaction of incredible vulnerability one shared with everything. I had seen that my home was now a prison and this had taught me to leap back into everything I had done in the name of art.

In the case of the hospital, which grew like a mechanical bush on a field, no one seemed able to recall a Paradise that had once been there and had vanished.

And yet – in my leap into works of art I had done – I perceived a Presence or an Atmosphere dwelling there in that bush. It seemed superior to me, to everyone I knew. That Presence inspected what had been lost in variable, well-nigh vanished traceries, it could still see with eyes on a leaf or a branch through the haze that lay everywhere.

Quetzalcoatl had been diminished across the ages. But sub-conscious/unconscious rumours and traceries persisted, some beautiful, some very perverse in the Atmosphere of a Lost Paradise where the ancient god was to be reborn.

Sometimes in the early mornings, or just before sunset, a flight of quetzal-parrots brought an echo of distant music from far overhead. Was this the annunciation of extinction or of rebirth? A deadly choice for the womb of Mankind: one that grew with the passing of every day and every year. I sought to paint the annunciation in zero-masks on the walls of my prison like echoing tendrils of flying Silences one heard in one's mind in the music of the Sky. Was this the murmur of paradisaical birds painted on a butterfly's wing that was stained as well with the blood of a misrepresented Serpent that – it was said – had broken Adam's and Eve's innocence in Paradise? This perverse rumour of a misrepresented Serpent, *coatl*, had become a fixed and popular legend. It ran into contrast with the peculiar Myth, on the walls of my cell, which gave one a glance into the infinite womb of nature in which no creature was absolute even though the Cyclopean guard held watch over the prisoners in their cells.

Quetzalcoatl, Bird and Serpent, was a vulnerable god in the unconscious of Mankind.

In the unconscious of Mankind, in the ancient and the modern.

This came to me with such startling and overwhelming immediacy it made me see the intricate terrains of works I had done in new and unsuspected lights – the terrain of Imagination into which I had now distinctly entered in meaningful, far-reaching deceptions of place that lifted me into walled otherness and into peculiar, changing sameness as though I were both in my studio and in a prison that had been my home, as though I were living consciousness and yet even more alive, it seemed, in a depth of original unconsciousness flowing into fragmentary, modern consciousness in sculptures and paintings and walls on which I could trace my ageing, youthful selves; the terrain of Lazarus as Man and as Atmosphere that conceals the radiancy of Myth in Rain and in Cloud; the terrain of hidden sculptures I had woven which were returning in fragmentary ways; the terrain of lost or stolen voices; the terrain of Carnival figurations; the terrain of Brides and Mothers of Space, large as life and miniature on a windowpane; the terrain of Angels out of visionary, neglected elements in the past – all these and more came into my mind with overwhelming but subtle power. I saw that civilization had little or no vision of the creative and re-creative, unfinished play of the unconscious in the mystery of consciousness. There were logical speeches about the unconscious but such logic – significant as it was – did not enter creative and re-creative and still more creative and re-creative, unfinished dimensions of the unconscious/conscious interplay of languages that otherwise become cells from which one must break or in which one must perish.

Now I was helped by the god of the unconscious, by fragments I could recall flowing into consciousness, to see afresh aspects of the reclining woman – the 'drugged woman', as she was called by the prison authorities – as she passed me in the corridor of the prison on a stretcher on her way to hospital to give birth to fragments which had long been buried in the very unconscious that assisted me, wryly and curiously, to see her as ancient and modern. It was an overturning, a re-assembly, an underturning, an indestructibility, of great Myth. I saw an unfinished relationship with the sculpture of the Mother of Space I had intuitively attempted.

I saw her black, holed eyes. They stared through me and beyond me. They spoke without speaking. They were strange and intimate. Was she flesh-and-blood or was she the animation of an impossible sculpture? One is confused by the life of the unconscious even though one thinks one knows . . . One is confused – her eyes seemed to say – by the speech of the Imagination in which one thinks one controls the language of things. At the end of the nineteenth century scientists thought they had the meaning of science – apart from a few frills still to be ironed out – but with the twentieth century, relativity and quantum physics blew a hole in their claim. Ends seem to have been reached before – her eyes seemed to say – but they have been blown apart into new beginnings. When did the universe begin? The fossil theory of evolution is in conflict with biblical charts of creation and people are still divided in schools and universities. The unconscious plays havoc with closures and with absolutes that one needs to see again and again and again with vulnerable eyes appointing open-minded vistas within oneself and beyond oneself. Does the universe expand and contract? Scientists were dumbfounded when they learnt it appears to be expanding ceaselessly.

I was lost in her eyes as in a picture I could barely imagine, a picture of the womb of nature.

Her face and her head were much larger than I had expected as though she were looking at me from a great height – even as she lay on her side, like a diagrammatic building on a sheet of paper – as she passed slowly on her stretcher. What height was this, what elevation? Was this a modern, technological diagram I had projected onto her, or was it an ancient elevation of body and mind that gave us both access to qualities of pictorial and inestimable scale?

There was a serenity that troubled me deeply in the expression of her features and in the picture of her mind, in her eyes, that spoke to me. A sombre serenity. It seemed to witness, not to beauty, in a Western sense, but to contrasting weathers of psyche that had left their mark on her.

Beauty is absolute, the great poet Keats declares: 'Beauty is truth,' but in her eyes this was an illusion. 'Beauty is a cover for Conquest,' she seemed to imply. Conquest signifies cruelties that pass muster under a haze. The conquistador is both savage and sophisticated. He brings fearful dominations from the culture he appears to own and passes them on to weaker cultures he now rules. Then he claims an Innocence for himself. Is Innocence an illusion?

All at once I was struck by the suggestion that *she* would rescue me not *I* her. She had said this before when I spoke with her in her cell. It left me helpless, uneasy, *guilty*, uncertain of who I was.

Guilt requires Imagination and Imagination is singularly absent from the various parties in our civilization. The Birth of a Child is seen as a local and a private event. Yet the newborn Child – in Its unconscious ancientness – is aware, more than an adult, of Itself as linked to others, despite Its pigmentation or race.

A Child carries a picture in Its mind, a living picture which we rarely see. The mind is 'It', the picture is 'It'.

A Child that is born in a prosperous state *knows*, without knowing, that it carries a stigma on the picture of Its mind. Hundreds of thousands, millions, are born and die of starvation in a poor, disadvantaged state. They are 'things' we do not see. That knowledge soon vanishes, the picture is hidden in the unconscious. A division robs the mind of an 'Itness' on which the guilt of a civilization resides.

Am I myself unimaginative as a bland lawyer or judge? Do I have great difficulty in seeing through an order of the law that someone who is ill, ill from the neck down, paralysed, unable to move, and who requests that he should die by a hand other than his own – since he cannot move his own – should *not* be allowed his or her request? His absolute, legal status is used to kill an unconscious/conscious desire that reaches beyond himself, to kill the 'Itness' of the mind, to kill an Imagination of a world to which he is linked through many, many others who die like 'things' in war, in violence, in the sentence of death imposed by a powerful state.

Do I help to nullify the picture by a lack of Imagination until nothing exists but an individual being, valueless, but innocent as ever?

The guilt of a civilization is hidden, except in the reality of Dreams, where self-portraits are woven, and instantly forgotten.

Then I knew – imaginative and unimaginative, knowing and unknowing – that I was becoming aware, however darkly, that the reclining woman, passing on a stretcher, was diagrammatically composed of unfixed pictures I thought I knew but which remained in a Dream, the journey of a Dream into the unconscious. The unconscious is a Jester with a bell, who is contemptuous of accumulations of knowledge, that we gain from a veneer of consciousness, from which a flowing, uncomfortable depth has been excluded. We may build castles of certainty but these are flattened in a flash and we start painfully erecting them all over again.

The suggestion that she was rescuing me – absurd as it was

for a woman as weak as she was – became loud and clear as a bell within a fragmented self-portrait I had begun whose ears I painted as muffled. Clarity of sound is uncertain.

The bell was still the 'Itness' of the mind despite its voicelessness. There were diagrammatic proportions in its ringing soundlessness of Dream that possessed features I had pursued but forgotten.

She lay on her right. Her left arm was bent over her side and it formed a triangle with a blackened line of her body. Her feet were arched, the burnt limbs of a tree, burning, not burning, into another triangle . . .

Here, I felt, was the intricate, living spell of a Forest that had been home to many species and was now destroyed. I was now that spell in the Journey of a Dream. Time lapses. Centuries are still. They are a Moment or a Picture of a bell that has no voice.

Her right arm lay under her raised head, raised from the stretcher, and it made another blackened line that formed a narrow rectangle beneath her head. Everything was still, no voice, but then I heard her cry with her black, holed eyes that were burning and not burning. The Forest or the home of Quetzalcoatlan species was burning and not burning.

This fire and non-fire was a joint veil that slipped out of the diagrammatic proportions of the woman on the stretcher. She was weak but she possessed values I had pursued in the Mother of Space, the Bride of Space. The veil fell around me like a robe in my Dream. I was now equipped, it seemed, to make the Journey that lay within me and beyond me. I could not tell what the veil or the robe signified other than a contrasting, furious element, fire and non-fire. I would have to learn more, much more . . . I could not tell . . . It seemed nevertheless immensely important. It was a substance one tastes with one's skin, with one's body, with one's inner/outer flesh, but cannot identify ... It was the reality of unconscious Dream flowing into uncertain consciousness.

'*Play Quetzalcoatl*,' her eyes cried out to me. '*Let him rise in you from me. He is my Child*. This is a terrifying business, I know. Shall I call it a "business"? Lame word. But there you are! To play a part that must – if it is played true – carry the stigmata of civilization, the marks, the terrors of centuries, is beyond local Birth. The Child of one art becomes the Child of other arts. And surely you can attempt to play such a varied part. Cortez was chosen by the ancient Mexicans. Cortez, the conquistador! How can the present time truly come alive, how can it be born or reborn, without participating profoundly in the catastrophes of the past? The ancient Mexicans made a ritual, dogmatic blunder in choosing Cortez. *Ritual, yes, dogmatic, yes*. We write our fictions like that. Are our fictions and our arts influenced by a people we conquered and humiliated? Do we not use their ritual, do we not use their dogma? Unconsciously we do. This has lain on us across five hundred years. It has grown into disasters, it has wasted our forests, it is killing our species – are they *our* species? – it has become a form of endemic violence and the lure of a mad invulnerability...'

Her holed eyes went on and I could not see what they were writing for me. I was amazed. I was stunned. I wanted to laugh. The laughter of the mind is a cure for ignorance. In losing the voice of the Mother of Space I had lost something that spoke from me, in me, in her. I became an acutely vulnerable god and artist. *I became the son of the unconscious with parts of consciousness affected very deeply by range and depth.* And so her eyes were crying to me and I was utterly astonished by the Silence of sound. What those eyes implied lay not in me as before but beyond me.

Was this a preparation for the Journey of Dream on which a civilization must embark to save itself before it is too late?

What face did Quetzalcoatl have? What did he look like? There are legends of bearded, white pictures, with white faces, born from a womb of bias. There are other legends of red fires, brown fires, blue fires like the Sky, dark fires, burning, not burning, in other faces, other furies, modulated perhaps, all of which he still resented.

He had no face. He was a *Nobody*, he was *Faceless*. And yet these strange features, fissured, broken, like the Mask of the Beggar I saw in West Street, as a Child, gave him an immense cross-culturality that reminded me of the veil I needed to understand.

7

The Journey of Dream was a self-portrait of staggering proportions. I participated in others, they participated in me. Even when they appeared individual and wholly different I still sensed a profound, unclear relationship. This came from an inward, underground, unexpected clarity, or semblance of clarity, or inexplicable clarity, that made me see myself more deeply, with greater certainty, with greater uncertainty, than I had known in and of myself before. Who was I, where was I going, where had I come from?

Was Comrade Stalin – what a Comrade was he – a conquistadorial Cortez of revolutionary Russia? A strange but true combination of terms. So it seemed to me.

Cortez had destroyed ancient Mexico. He had destroyed precious books and arts, the bloodstream of a way of life. He had employed guns like monstrous, living but insensible things he touched and fired but did not know. He had extinguished the distinction of gods who ministered to fate, who opened doors beyond fate, into the Sun and into the stars. He had learnt nothing except a ritual and a dogma that made the ancient Mexicans see him as a returning Quetzalcoatl. The only god he appeared to know was that of the horse on which he sat like a half-man, a half-demon. And yet he worshipped the Church of Rome at which all were forced into absolute obedience without conscience or creativity.

Comrade Stalin destroyed the revolutionary hopes of Russia. He employed ritual and dogma as an implacable weapon with which to hunt to extinction all who dared to think their own thoughts and to give expression to their dreams. He tracked 'revolution' where it was least seen. He tracked the concept of a 'permanent revolution', a 'world revolution', across continents into Mexico where Trotsky had arrived. Such a concept was a rare possibility but a dangerous hope that baffled thinkers and ideologues. But Comrade Conquistador took no chances. He despatched an assassin to Mexico. Trotsky was murdered in 1940.

A 'stilled' portrait of Trotsky, that touched my self-portrait in its veiled dimensions, brings him to Harbourtown in the year 2000. This was the year when Quetzalcoatl sprang afresh in the prison hospital from the diagrammatic proportions of the Mother of Space: a spring that signified terrible happenings, terrible traces of sins to be investigated in ways that would expose and possibly transfigure a state of endemic violence in a civilization. He sprang, it seemed, in my Journey of Dream, like a tall Child, a grown Child in me and in Quetzalcoatl whom I identified with a Child and with an unconscious father. Father and Child! Such is the logic or illogic of Dream. He sprang from a weak mother, wasted limbs, wasted forests, wasted creation, root and branch mirroring our ignorance of beginnings and endings. Weakness was the best I could achieve across years of work that led to the Journey of Dream on which I was now embarked. A weakness that bore a frail resemblance nevertheless to the strong, Olympian god Zeus, from whose head (or diagram, as it may have appeared, to the other gods on Olympus) was born Pallas Athene, full-blown, a woman, a goddess of wisdom and of war. Wisdom seemed native to war, war to wisdom, in the evolution of human faces in the arts of the world.

Was Pallas a 'stilled' portrait in terms of her birth from a father rather than a mother? Was Quetzalcoatl an ambiguous figure in terms of a fatherhood and a childhood he carried in himself in his resentment of a Face, a fixed Face, whether young or old?

They are both 'stilled' portraits and 'stilled' portraits – whether from weak mothers or strong fathers, whether as child and unconscious father at the same mysterious, evolving moment – cannot be trusted. They are the denizens of Dream. They are woven in fear and misgiving. Yet they flow from indestructible Myth.

One may seek to abandon them and to concentrate exclusively on the present, on present limbs, present factualities, present, illusory wholeness. But they bring reminders or traces of a past we cannot entirely abandon even though we push Time into the unconscious and hope it will rest there and pass into Nothingness.

The Journey of Dream commences with Nothingness, with Nobody and Faceless; it probes into the unconscious, where much is hidden, and the 'stilled' portraits are aroused. They may come in murdered forms, or as murderers, to expose and transfigure what has happened in the past.

They (those 'stilled' portraits) join together and speak of things we have preserved as finished events. We hope thereby to lose the 'uncreativity' of deeds that become statistics in the News of history.

Did Comrade Stalin have an 'uncreative' hand in the massacre of Nicholas II, the emperor of Russia, and his family by the Red Guards in 1918 at Ekaterinburg?

Did the conquistador Cortez bring about the 'uncreativity' that killed the last emperor of Mexico, Montezuma II, in 1520?

Quetzalcoatl may appear as ruthless as Cortez, as ruthless as *Nobody* who blinded the Cyclops and enraged Poseidon, the god of the sea, who was the father of the Cyclops.

Such ruthlessness is cross-cultural. It touches on the

'uncreativity' of fathers who claim they determine the absolute origins of Spirit. It touches on Myth and the well-nigh silent word that speaks of many escapes from determined factualities. There are unrecognized edges, there are subtle openings, there are escapes from fatality, revengeful fatherhood, which may be indiscernible in one culture alone.

I stopped and pondered and asked myself: is this the meaning of the Veil? Is this a hidden attribute of weakness, we rarely see, which combines one culture with another through diagrams, zero-diagrams? I shall wait and see. Perhaps the word 'weakness' is inappropriate in discussing the nature(s) of vulnerability, which occupies the strongest amongst us. The strongest are vulnerable . . .

Quetzalcoatl employs the Bird and the Snake as symbols of winged and swift escape into a Spirit that broods over many creations, many universes. He takes into himself – in my dreaming, fragmented self-portrait – all questions that deal with a reluctance to accept a human Face as absolutely his. The Face of Man is corrupt however honest and smooth it appears.

I had sensed this extreme reluctance – if 'sense' is the word – within my overturned, upturned Self that was mirrored in those of whom I dreamt, within my mythic self-portrait, when I placed Quetzalcoatl – as a hidden master of the globe – on a plinth with six or seven companions, one of whom was a woman. Did such reluctance expose a desire in me to hide from a truly creative and conscience-aroused reality? The men wore zero-masks that pinned their faces into holed openings in a sliding, uncomfortable way. The woman I could not properly see. Was she Quetzalcoatl's sister, his mistress, his wife? The masks were uncomfortable. They slid and revealed – in a partial degree – the universal Faces of Man.

I had hidden this sculpture away in my studio. It was

agonizing, quantum truth with multiple variations. I was no master of the globe but the past rose in me as much as it did in them who had ruled and lost the world in 'uncreative' ways I accepted as normal. They descended on a ladder, in my Dream, from the plinth. Their wooden, iron dress clattered into flesh-and-blood. How could I identify with them? Such is the logic, or illogic, of Dream.

In a capitalist economy such logic or illogic is clear. Such translations into flesh-and-blood are clear. Technology speaks. Weaponry speaks. The institutions of a ruthless marketplace gain more and more supremacy. They aim to pay high wages to the workers who must, as a consequence, surrender their independence, or conscience, in fostering greater and greater profits for the institutions that employ them . . . The Journey of Dream is more native to the world in which we live than a blind factuality that does not see beyond a money-making, political order of things . . .

Who descends from my plinth in the Dream? Is it the old conquistadorial devils? Is it 'uncreativity' masquerading as military revolution? Is it one or many? Are there subtle edges in the fabric of the Veil? Cold-hearted flesh-and-blood they seem, one or many . . . The zero-masks slide. Cortez, Pizarro, Stalin, Nicolas II, Montezuma II, Trotsky . . .

Quetzalcoatl is not amongst them. He *knows* that his Face, whatever Face he wears, modern or ancient, is a disguise. He is a vulnerable god. He senses – darkly perhaps – that the Veil possesses subtle openings which must be investigated in range and depth to gain an entrance into different worlds even in this.

I was left in a state of amazement. I still did not fathom the purposes of the Veil. Had the masters of the globe seen *through* themselves, *into* themselves, *beyond* themselves? This seemed a virtual impossibility. But one could never tell.

I saw them as still clothed, however dismantled they seemed, in the *blindness* of ritual murder, the dogma of murder in the killing of those one loathes, whom one feels have executed crimes, great or small. It was a *blindness* that divides the world into good, which one stands for, and into evil, which the others one has condemned, stand for.

I saw Cortez clothed in the ritual and the dogma of murder but with an expression that brought home to me my innermost responsibility as an artist for him as a master of the globe. Do I not speak of him in history books? What is the art of mastery? Do masters exist by themselves above myth and its strange warnings of a wholeness we must strive for endlessly perhaps?

He looked now, I felt, as if he wore a semblance of the Mask of the Beggar I had seen as a Child in West Street. His expression – that brought home to me a complex self-portrait across the centuries involving, amongst others, an alien commander and conquistador – was fissured and broken into dots, curves and bones. A 'stilled' portrait, wrapped in meaningful reality and illusion, timeless, timely. Was this the irony of mastery? He stood now above Tenochtitlan (which is now Mexico City in modern Mexico). He stood now, like a skeleton of moving land in mist and haze, beside the volcanoes, *The Sleeping Lady* and *Popocatapetl the Warrior*. It was from here that he had descended on Tenochtitlan centuries ago.

In his *blind* conviction of himself as eternally good – an eternal goodness that ignored the Mask of the Beggar in which the others, whom he loathed and condemned, issued from the crevices in his Face (or lack of Face) – he seemed to appeal to the Sleeping Lady – asleep yet inwardly and volcanically alive – who may have been Quetzalcoatl's sister in the sculpture of Quetzalcoatl and his six companions and a woman in my studio. The mists and the haze made them all seem to be there high above Tenochtitlan.

What a cross-cultural signal of remorse was this that struck a deep, sounding chord in me . . .

Was he conscious of the flow of the unconscious into the *hollow* face he turned to me? Was he conscious of himself as *hollow* in a dressed picture of history to which he clung, and to which I seemed to cling, to which democracies – as hollow as he – clung?

Cortez had displaced himself in a 'stilled' portrait, wrapped around a skeleton of mist, which had travelled from 1520, in ancient Mexico, back to the Cyclops and the Beggar, in a dark Time, and forwards still to the year 2000 which was darker still than Homer's age.

Dreams cannot be trusted. They are wry, bitter parables. But they are essential guides into our blindness to pasts and futures. Humanity is spiritually blind. That blindness varies, changes a little, gives us partial glimpses through 'stilled' portraits that we encounter in Dream. If we accept our age as plagued with blindness, as more plagued than Man was in previous times, we have a chance, it seems, of seeing ancient particulars (we never truly understood) in a new, revealing, universal (however partial) light. Light is filled with haze – obvious haze, haze that seems a clarity – which baffles the strongest, physical vision. All this, universal and partial, may help us to understand the new, hidden particulars of our age with their roots nevertheless in an ancient, *living* soil.

The varied and various lives of the soil are priceless. They cry out in several tongues we scarcely understand for many approaches to the unconscious, to the conscious gradients of Man who treads the Earth, to the mist of his breath on fire and water. When one begins to see *creatively* the varied life of the Earth through oneself it brings one into touch with uncanny universes one shares with the unseen and the seen.

Had the ancient Mexicans *perceived creatively* the life of the soil in the midst of ritualistic and dogmatic codes of material changelessness? They saw, but their interpretations of what they saw left them confused ... They saw before I begin to see ... It is difficult, I know to approach the life of the Earth in contrasting particulars that bear on the mystery of wholeness when wholeness itself seems precarious and may not endure in an idiom one takes for granted. Everything seems clear in that idiom except the trap of fate it conceals.

Because of this dilemma I knew I was partially awake, in my Journey of Dream, to the seeming mist of the Skeleton, and could inspect my self-portrait with humour and in a sober perhaps dispassionate light through Cortez's dressed appearance. Had he dressed himself around a mist? What is 'himself'? Does it differ from the Skeleton? Was the 'dress' he wore the illusory gift of Quetzalcoatl's physical appearance and disappearance? In Quetzalcoatl's birth and rebirth he appeared and disappeared. Such is the varied law of universal Spirit. Nothing was absolute. Nothing could be taken for granted in language or imagery however persuasive it may appear at one stage of tradition.

Equally – in such a context of waking and sleeping, appearance and disappearance – I felt the frail life of Cortez as a summons of universal conscience. He was alive beside the volcanoes, one of war, the other of a womb that broke through all assumptions and needed to be courted and worshipped with the greatest care. Such was ancient Mexican religion, the courtship and the worship of living, precarious natures.

The life of Cortez, it seemed, was that of a frail consciousness between contrasting natures. He was reborn unwittingly as conscience from enemy-particulars, from Mexican-particulars.

This paradox broke the boundaries of his blindness. So it seemed to me in my cross-cultural self-portrait. He sprang from war but held unwittingly to the Sleeping Lady or womb of underground, majestic upheaval that rose into the Sun in Mexico's high volcanoes.

> Who was the Sleeping Lady in Harbourtown?
> She rose as well from the Shang Mountain.

She was asleep there yet interiorly active in the arts I pursued. Shang Mountain lay in the interior of Harbourtown and presaged a marriage between Trotsky, a 'permanent revolutionary', and a Chinese Immigrant. That marriage was prepared in a Bridal, miniature Cup that an Oriental Sage held in his hand in my studio. A preparation I had not fully considered by any means. *Now* it shook me, it amazed me. *I had painted the new life of Cortez in a quantum variation in which I saw the acute misgivings that arose in him for the first time in my art.* He had awakened to the enemy-particulars from which he came back to life. He could hardly bear such a revelation and he held an ice-pick of dazzling light in one hand, with which he stabbed Trotsky in the brain, a misty brain perhaps after centuries, but shaped like a Cup of blood in the hand of the Oriental Sage . . .

Quantum variations move and change fixed idioms, in a twentieth-century world so absolutely entrenched, none may see connections between an Oriental, pre-Columbian Sage – who held a Cup of blood in one hand as a Bridal Chamber between many warring cultures – and Cortez with a misty ice-pick with which he stabbed Trotsky on the heights above Tenochtitlan and Harbourtown.

The assassin Stalin had sent had used an ice-pick in stabbing Trotsky. I used painted light. Light freezes in weapons of war and in cups or bowls or in technologies, which seem harmless, with which we cut or slice cake or ice for dinner. The cannibalism of war dies hard. Bullets freeze. Bombs freeze. Our hands freeze or turn to vanished, re-appearing mist. We are involuntary assassins. We eat meals and hide the weapons that we use to eat. We are conditioned by a nameless feud between man and man we have never penetrated or understood. A feud with the Sun, with the stars, with lights and darknesses which we appoint as our targets. Our appointment of such targets requires a human, transfigurative art we have never understood. We obey obscure masters of the globe who may be traced backwards in Space and Time like a fury or a star or an energy at the edge of the universe. Such furies keep the feud alive but they wait for us to hear their disconsolate misgivings and dismay in the reaches of Time and Space.

I am caught in my art within an unfathomable Spirituality that bends and moves and shifts to accommodate my failings – as a god and an artist – and to give hope to my possibilities. The enmities that are displayed may become the source of a far-reaching, cross-cultural wisdom.

Cortez cried in his dismay and acute misgiving that seemed to come from above Harbourtown and Tenochtitlan: 'I did not stab Trotsky from my perch above Tenochtitlan. This is an outrageous Dream . . .'

'You did,' I insisted. 'When you killed ancient Mexico – when you killed the Earth-Sun that they worshipped – you set in train a series of trails that led to the murder of Trotsky four hundred years later. Light freezes and makes us blind until we see its cross-cultural proportions across ages.'

I was dumbfounded and confused even as I spoke. Who was I to have a deep understanding of ancient Mexico? Cortez and the conquistadors had burnt and destroyed much that was invaluable. And yet I clung to the little that I knew since it brought Cortez back to life in my paintings, the Cortez who was master of the globe I had inherited through the Conquest in which he broke a profound and significant culture into pieces. Quantum pieces I would say. They offered the only way of reconciling opposites, Death and Life, Cortez (the dead master), Cortez (the living, awakening conscience).

Do gods and artists inherit the blind mastery of ruthless men? Do they deceive themselves when these masters, and their descendants, corner a fund of knowledge that seems factual or scientific? Do they inherit mind-sets that place a settled idiom upon interpretation until interpretation is mistaken for fact, the mystery of fact?

The Sun was shining in the haze and mist upon the heights of Harbourtown and Tenochtitlan, heights that seemed a plinth above the floor in my studio. The floor was the surface of the Earth in miniature. How to interpret Shang Mountain (which is a miniature fact) and the Sleeping Lady on Tenochtitlan (which is also a miniature fact) in my studio? Some interpretations claim they are dissimilar but as miniatures in my studio they approach cosmic, hidden, variable Space and are drawn together into a placeless or enigmatic similarity. Cortez (dead yet tormentingly alive in cosmic Space) is imbued with the volcanic nature of the Sleeping Lady on an Earth-plane of a cultural validity he seems to have destroyed. He is imbued with a sliding, underground nature which reaches across a continent and a globe with plates that move and come together to give utterance to an upheaval that sounds from place to place like blind/singing players in a theatre that is never closed but ceaselessly open to quantum similarities of indescribable music.

For decades the plates that move beneath the Earth were rejected by science, which was deaf on surfaces to their music. Even now the interpretations of the plates is little understood in forms of art. Art deals with vulnerability in the mystery of fact. Fact is miniature in cosmic Space however large it may seem in our entrenched situations. The volcanic upheaval of the Sleeping Lady gives Cortez the sensation of distant furies to be modified or modulated within the intimate heart and body of Man whom I paint as a spectrum of infinity. One paints phantasms of fact. In such phantasms one hopes to draw a little closer to the mystery of fact in unfathomable Spirit, one hopes to draw closer to interpretation that changes its quantum direction into amazing correspondences. Who can plumb the Silences of the distant stars like pin-pricks far back in Space and Time? We may interpret them as large as we wish but all interpretation is open to weird and still more weird, unfinished fact.

The heights on which I saw Cortez became a dazzling Zero. They formed a numinous and basic instance I hardly understood of consciousness playing through a door in a Veil. His 'stilled' portrait moved through that sliding Sun or Zero. He emerged, it seemed, within a tumult of 'war' and 'womb', Popocatapetl and the Sleeping Lady.

Which was more native to history? 'War' was a continuing practice, the 'womb' was an upheaval within the 'sleep' of sculptures in my studio. 'Sex' was a 'sleep' and it led to dire consequences of innumerable, unwanted 'births' around the globe. Here was, I felt, the terrifying dichotomy of ancient Mexican civilization that 'awoke' from a 'sleep' in their arts and gods (miniaturized in my studio) into the life of natures projected into the precariousness of the Sun. The gods awoke with a sense of acute terror. They fell back on religious ritual and dogma. They (through priests) were persuaded that the 'heart' of selected victims was the food of demanding nature.

The Sun was alive, precariously alive, they felt, and it needed to be nourished or the Earth would perish.

Dogma was restrictive and cruel but once opened into inner necessities and variations it could have provided conquistadorial Europe with the life of the Earth which it has taken close on five hundred years to begin to see. It could have led to a New, Cross-Cultural World in the sixteenth century in the midst of the jolting and terrible reality of the life of the Sun as a numinous and factual Zero in a Veil...

I was startled by this. It left me puzzled and uncertain. *Was Zero a numinous spirit rather than a savage number? Did it bring Cortez to life through the Veil?*

Cortez was alive. I still could not accept this. I had trailed into philosophical arguments to avoid the fact of a life in which a remorse came into play for the deeds performed in the past. This remorse was plain. 'Not so plain!' I told myself. He carried an ice-pick (with which he had stabbed Trotsky), a gun, a bomb. It was as if a metal arm had grown across the centuries with which he automatically slew his opponents, or with which he was sent by others as an involuntary assassin. But his other arm, almost shrunken into a tender extension of his frailty, gave him (*gave me*) a sensation of inner vulnerability. However metallically strong he was, he could not avoid a feeling of tender weakness in my Journey of Dream. This tenderness opened into a window through which he looked *through* himself, *beyond* himself, through me, beyond me.

I was deeply confused by the life of frail consciousness returning across the centuries. I could not believe *I* would so return. *I* was affected, gravely affected. Could *I* (whoever I was) change? Could I relearn myself in a future that bears on the past, relearn metallic guilt and tenderness? *Was this relearning a miracle of art?*

How could a ruthless dictator – in whom I embodied myself in Dream – come back to life in agonized, remorseful forms still committed to violence, because of a metallic arm, but deeply agonized into re-creative tenderness?

It was impossible. It signified a phenomenon of mysterious factuality and fiction. It signified a mutuality between moving opposites in the depths of the human psyche I still could not accept. Opposites were absolutely identified with a blow of violence which one side or the other would administer in war or terrorism. They were not identified with the moving plates beneath the Earth's surface that could assist us to plan settlements with some degree of safety.

Violence was all conventional art knew. *Now, however, I saw Cortez, a bodily/bodiless master of the globe, with raised hands (akin to mine when I was a Child), one as violent as ever, in the metallic twentieth century, the other as a re-visionary mind – hand as mind – reaching out beyond domination into the modulation of the furies of the world.*

'Impossible,' I said.

What did Cortez look like? What did *I* look like? Were we Muslim, was *I* white American, was he black or white African, was I Asian, was he European, had he (or I) returned again in one of the faces of another deceptive arrival of Quetzalcoatl? I could not tell. The mist and sun were half-dazzling on Shang Mountain. The figures there puzzled my heart. I saw the metallic arm in the dazzling sunlight, I saw the tender, shrunken mind ... They were part of a phantasm of fact in my age. Or was it Quetzalcoatl's gift of opposites, blending by creative and re-creative degrees into one another, to assume an art of Spirit that could change the world within self-portraitures that were ceaseless, always unfinished, always edged by otherness?

The miniature figure of Cortez stood close to Popocatapetl the Warrior and looked down on Tenochtitlan. The glorious city he remembered had vanished. Memory persists in a master of the globe but makes its poignancy deeply felt in all that has vanished.

The beautiful canals, the bridges, had vanished. I tried to paint them but saw them only on the back of a Serpent with marvellous triangles and stripes sliding down Shang Mountain.

He remembered the awe and the wonder with which he had gazed on Tenochtitlan when he first arrived. The remembered awe and wonder he had felt then – which he still felt now for vanished glories – frightened him. The confusing serpentine coils of light slipped away beneath him in my paint. The Serpent is a mystery of nature on which one deposits one's inner greeds, one's inner passions, to possess all that one sees.

One latches on to nothing save material wealth and gold. He saw this now as a sliding coil he had partially overcome, a deadly bias and a blindness with which one conquers the world.

Had anything really changed? He saw change, in some degree, but he was uncertain whether it was seen at all as a universal problem. Tenochtitlan and Shang Mountain, however apparently distant from each other, were united by insignificant-seeming players in a theatre of the depths and heights one did not truly understand. Those players, for instance, were birds and serpents in the gods of ancient Mexico. Birds and serpents disappear and reappear in human dress. It is an art to be carefully pursued. Such arts speak of the mystery of all natures. They speak of terror and greed and tragedy and pity from which no one is immune. It was a question of identities that seem both illusory and real in pointing to a time *beyond* material fallacies.

Did ancient Mexico have a solution? If it did it has been destroyed by the conquistadors but it remains a tantalizing, living issue in Quetzalcoatl.

Cortez remembered the markets brimming with scales of gold, with lines of silver, precious jewels like starry numbers, bright-seeming feathers, when he descended from Popocatepetl and came amongst them. I descended too in my Journey of Dream from Shang Mountain into Harbourtown.

He (and I, the Dreamer) remembered the magnificently shaped temples and Montezuma's luxurious palaces sliding, it seemed, into a doom no one yet understood.

Why 'doom'? Everything was bright. All that Montezuma needed was to practise what Cortez would teach him, to abstain from sacrifices in which still-beating hearts were offered to a living, precarious Sun... If Montezuma were obedient in this and in everything else of value, it seemed, that Cortez brought with him *to contain and imprison the people*, 'doom' would be avoided but if not Montezuma would pay with his life for persisting in his 'savagery'.

Cortez brought a god with him, an art with him, that was incorrigibly divine, god and artist! How incorrigible, how divine? It was a question I would have to answer in proving the values of art. It lay with me across the years as an artist and a god myself...

It rang a bell in me and I painted Cortez – in an extension of my self-portrait – as a quantum master breaking out, in some degree, from his prejudices and from mine. But I could not wholly cast off the ancient, unconscious/subconscious desire to master the globe that *persisted as the real savagery in all times from Alexander the Great through Napoleon to Hitler and Mussolini.*

Gold may have slipped innocently from the Serpent's back in ancient Mexico, or from a Bird's wing, but it was destined to pass mechanically from hand to hand and he (Cortez) would control all hands in his. Gold was no longer to be measured in a Serpent's scale. *Gold was Money.*

Had I succumbed automatically to such a mercenary creed that sacrificed the intimacy of animals to Man's mechanical desires?

I had pursued this for years, in many variations, after I came upon the Beggar I loathed and loved in West Street and had raised a hand to my mouth but could not eat. Whose hand was it that I raised in imitative protest at Cortez's creed? Was it a hand I plucked, without knowing, from the Beggar's fissured Mask? One acts and does not know what memory, hidden in ourselves and others, drives us to do.

Now this confusing action was emerging all over again but partly seen, I felt, partly understood this time. Perhaps I had brought this partial and deep, confused understanding to light, in different ways, in my intuitive arts. I had slung the painted mantle of Cortez on my back and felt a hollow bleakness within me I had never known before. Such hollowness, such bleakness, in a master of the globe. It made me feel Quetzalcoatl's immensely disturbing, unsatisfied Face in my paint as Cortez – claiming to be Quetzalcoatl – approached Montezuma in remembered Tenochtitlan. He had a knife in his hand raised and still. Was it a confused desire to kill and not to kill Montezuma?

Montezuma saw nothing in the darkness of Time. He welcomed Cortez seeing Quetzalcoatl in him returning across the Seas into which he had vanished. A supreme but dark opportunity for alien cultures, one from Europe, the other from ancient America, to open a door between them that had never been opened before. The knife Cortez carried had been lodged there pointing one way or another. The door was still ajar but my bleakness was terrifying. It seemed impossible, even now, to believe the knife in that door intended anything but a hand of violence...

I meditated on my abrupt, unfinished remarks and asked

myself: 'Where does an artist and a god, who is not incorrigible, who may be the son of an unfathomable Spirit, stand now in this bleak age of individualistic creeds that contain, at their core, the ancient mastery, through violence or hidden violence, of the globe?' A crude question, perhaps, but true. Does one not deceive oneself about real and true change affecting a universal and cross-cultural Mankind? Does one not deceive oneself about the savagery one carries in oneself alongside sensations of confusing possibilities of revelation lodged in one's hand as if one's hand is both one's own and another's?

Where do I stand in all such deceptions between myself and others? What 'stillness' do I seek, what 'stilled' direction in a moment of Time that returns again and again, however bleak, however terrifying?

This is the confession of an artist at a time when such confessions are needed. One tends to despair of the life of Spirit when man-made obstinacies do not see the 'novel' as 'new'.

Let me begin by saying that I am largely an intuitive writer. I find myself an astonished creation of forces that create me even as I appear to create them. 'I' and 'we' and 'one' and versions of these are such forces in this confession. What emerges late perhaps may help to deepen or clarify, in some degree, what appears earlier. The bridging of gaps is the mystery of consciousness. We have been intuitively seeking in this fiction hidden twinships and physicalities that are wholly neglected in creative complexity save in quantum variations (particle and wave) of the things civilization takes for granted.

We cannot take the Seas for granted.

We see ourselves travelling across a spirit of waters in which Quetzalcoatl vanished.

Did he vanish? Ancient Mexico invested in his return as the

West invests in the return of Christ from an empty grave and from the uncertain, creative and re-creative Veil of the land. How could they entirely vanish in a gap we still need to bridge in ourselves and others?

We know now that Quetzalcoatl – in hidden, intuitive form – was on the Ships that brought Immigrants from China into Harbourtown and South and Central America.

He is there in the early variations of this fiction but so hidden he appears not to be there at all.

The Ships go down but still sail in Space on the wave like stars of originality. That is Quetzalcoatlan astronomy and vision and it informs the entire work in hidden twinship with the Mask of the Beggar.

How do the Ships vanish, how do they coalesce in visionary shape and return? Such happenings lie beyond conventional language in silent imageries beneath the surface of the Earth and in Space.

They lie beyond ritual and dogma. They lie in realms beyond bland convention, which misses a diversity in wholeness, which misses spiritual bleakness and dangers in the feud of Man it has never sought to understand beyond the one-sided News of fact; it misses mutualities, dualities, ecstasies that grope into a marriage with infinity . . .

It may well be that this series of explorations is a 'failure' but this brings home to me that all our Faces – in the Quetzalcoatlan sense – are clothed in corruption. They may seem noble, or they may wear a panoply of success, but they conceal the intricate, far-reaching truths that art seeks.

The Ships to which I referred – with Immigrants crossing the Ocean in previous centuries – are so Time-bound, so located on or under an absolute wave, that they seem sunken to the Imagination (whatever roles they may have performed) and are unlikely to be visualized – in a spiralling Quetzalcoatlan re-vision – as prophetic of the submarine and the vessels which now haunt the Oceans of the world above and beneath. Are they (however newly invented) technological ghosts that corrupt the High Seas with litter and deadly cargoes? Or do they carry at this moment remorseful, re-creative tokens of a complexity that brings the past instinctually alive? The instinct of life in art arises from partial and inner recognitions (that are ceaseless) of the hidden in ourselves and others which can never be emptied of a content that varies in Space and Time.

What is 'instinct'? We have learnt by slow and painful degrees that the Earth is alive, it is 'instinct' with vulnerabilities. We too – however strong we may feel – possess 'windows' born of vulnerabilities in ourselves that allow us to see through ourselves, beyond ourselves. And thus we acquire a sensibility of wings in psyche or spirit that take us around the globe and into Space. Not by mechanical means which may leave us prone to travel without 'instinct' like tourists in a cage of glass devoid of self-portraitures that are edged into unfamiliar traces of wholeness. Not by such means but by a cross-cultural Imagination that may well be the first, ancient inkling of the arts, though we have neglected or forgotten its workings in the mind.

I speak here of an ancient and flexible substance of which we learn so erratically, so slowly, it is 'new' or 'novel' when it appears. The moving plates under the surface of the Earth have only recently been discovered though they have been active in shaping the very ground on which we live.

They may help us to combine in daring ways the surfaces of the Earth with underground and shifting physicalities – that affect the surfaces – which we have grossly neglected and which are necessary for the survival of life.

I have miniaturized Tenochtitlan and Harbourtown to gain some inkling of an urgency with which we may plan settlements more in tune with the nomadic wanderings of ancient peoples, in the native

Americas, and their escapes from fires or quakes or floods or droughts...

THERE WAS A CRASH. A large rock had been thrown from Water Street through the window of my studio and had crashed on the floor beside the map of Space. I rushed to the window and saw a man, barely five feet tall, standing in the Street. He was dressed in a most handsome suit and was staring up intently at me. He began to ascend from the Street to the door of my studio. The Sleeping Lady and Shang Mountain had been turned on their heads and the man came from below, it seemed, rather than from above. The Sky was in the Street not in the clouds...

Peoples in the distant past, who greeted us now in a bone or two found in the soil – not much different from figurine or miniature sculptures animated by outlines of travelling spirit – may have escaped quakes or fires or floods but the bottled-up and the upside-down furies, in the feud of Man, had brought surges of violence from which there was less predictable possibility of escape. Here, in such narrow predictability – as with the rigours of civilization – was a constriction (a prison) I experienced imaginatively in my 'stilled' and simultaneous activities in my studio and prison, a prison that replaced my home in West Street...

Within such 'stillness' – such traces of studio and prison and home – a radioactive Stone, it seems, comes into play from within a diverse Mankind united by bones of art. Unpredictable play. It demolishes communities, populations, around the Earth. I felt the danger threatening my sculptures and paintings. They were on the verge of demolition.

Scientists dwell on such catastrophes as a purely physical blow without a travelling Spirit. It demolished the dinosaurs, they tell us. And it is likely to strike again and wipe out

Mankind, wipe out the arts of Mankind before they reveal their complex and diverse universality. What a void this would signify in which antennae reach through shell into living, unconscious reality...

They (the scientists) make no provision for a numinous potential that breaches in secret and in Spirit (as is happening now in my studio) the tapestry of entrenched cultures unable to see or understand in re-creative linkage – without domination from one or the other – their festering points of view, festering imprisonments, festering, uneasy openness.

The numinous potential, the numinous explosion, hand-in-'stilled'-hand with the blow from the Sky, erupts or crashes, I feel, on the floor of my studio.

Do they indeed come together? Or does numinosity come first?

I pick up the Stone from the floor of my studio.

Cortez apparently vanishes from the upside-down Popocatapetl except for what seems a mantle of mist I had painted on his back and mine.

The large radioactive Stone also carries a map of the globe resembling the map on the floor. I see the Amazon descending from the Andes. I see the Mediterranean.

I look through Cortez's twisted bandage or mantle and see Quetzalcoatl's Face melting into mine and others. Montezuma had assumed that Cortez brought an incorrigible, divinely right Quetzalcoatlan Face across the Seas. Instead I see Lazarus's *Faceless* emergency as he arises from the grave and this is in league with Homer's *Nobody* escaping from the Cyclops. Has Lazarus defeated the Cyclops of death – at Christ's 'stilled' hand – by an allegiance to Homer's open-ended myth of Odysseus escaping from a symbolic tomb where he would have been eaten by the giant within...?

The man who had ascended from the Street (or descended from the Sky) had now entered my studio.

He was an eerie, unexpected man whom I had invited, it seemed, but whom I would have to struggle with to know. The light arising from the Street, in which the Sky moved, dazzled my sight. It seemed, all at once, that he was the living embodiment of burning, non-burning fires that had lit my studio from the beginning. He was an embodiment akin to the woman in the Street who was an exact likeness of the sculpted figure on the map of art in my studio. Except that – with light and fire and the beautiful suit that he wore – he seemed palpably inexact. He was a deceiver, I felt, an ageless deceiver, as old as Prometheus, who had brought fire from the gods, in their subjection to unfathomable Spirit. Had anyone solved the meaning of fire, fire as destroyer, fire as creator? Had I come a little closer to a solution with my deceiving visitor who was burning and yet not burning? Was he a spiritual spy, had he entered my studio, when I was absent, and rifled through my books?

Words stuck to my tongue. I wanted to say: 'Why did you throw the Stone?', but could not. Had I become an unspeaking/speaking sculpture in my own studio through which I imagined the traumas of wood as flesh, flesh as wood?

His trauma, I felt, was fire. He came from a world with which I wrestled intuitively in burning, non-burning lights that shone around me. Had that intuition come to a head at last? I could not tell. Men and women kill and burn themselves in order to kill and burn others.

Is this the sanity of wood?

Is it the madness of flesh?

I felt he would not burn me with the instinct he possessed for a non-burning/burning reality that sprang from below as much as from above. Upside-down furies help us to see a little better through our blindness... Help us to see the edges of Space wherever we are...

'Surely you know who I am?'

I shook my head, still tongue-tied like a piece of sculpture I had carved in my studio.

'*I am the Child-like man whom you rescued from prison.*'

He spoke in a matter-of-fact voice that could have been a deception he was playing on me. He was staring, as he spoke, at a book on a table in which I kept voluminous notes of sculptures and paintings I intended to make. I was shocked. My tongue was loosened.

'Rescued you?' I spoke with the inner voice of a sculpture. A deep, crackling, inner voice. I felt I suddenly understood why voices are stolen and why they arise from the pit of one's Imagination in extremities of sculpture and painting.

'You threw this very Stone that you hold in your hand now. It's carved with a map of the world. You threw it and you pierced a hole in the wall of the prison through which I ran before the guards could seize me... You also rescued the reclining woman and Lazarus...'

'*I did not rescue you,*' I said in a hoarse, almost unnatural voice that seemed unlike my real voice. 'I may have rescued Lazarus but the reclining woman rescued me and sent me out into Space and Time in a Journey of Dream. Dreams give us inner wings... You know certain half-truths from my notes. Are you a spy? *I did not rescue you.*'

I stopped in consternation. Had he read the book with voluminous notes? I suddenly remembered something I had forgotten in the inner pit of a strange Imagination. Had I not planned to rescue the Child-like man, had I not planned a good story-line based on a riot that had occurred in Harbourtown? It was a secret I kept from everyone. It was a secret, it seemed, of another age. With what light had he pierced the pages of a book compiling this age and other ages? *The book was a prison in which I kept matters that made me so dreadfully uneasy I had no option, it seemed, but to lock them away from others as others, in disguised sculpture or urbane flesh, locked them away from me.* The Child-like man was there in that book as a prisoner in a cell, who had attempted to swim an ocean – in Quetzalcoatlan form – but with whom I felt dreadfully uneasy. I had swum with him in my Imagination but eventually had consigned him to a book or prison of civilization. A book of voluminous, factual notes, it seemed, compiling many of which and whom I despaired, not understanding the grip of their Imaginations on me, my grip on them.

I was filled with consternation and guilt.

The man in the beautiful, London-cut, Paris-woven, New York-fired suit was laughing at me. He seemed to blaze a little. He was the light of eyes that came through the window of book and prison and studio in which the Stone had passed. Blind/seeing eyes, I thought, of deceiving Promethean/Quetzalcoatlan fire. They seemed to burn in him and not to burn. The light darkened and he darkened; it shone, he shone again. There was a riotous inclination in such a blaze.

'I have grown five feet tall,' he said, laughing still. 'I have grown from a miniature or a figurine in your book of notes. Have I grown into *true* flesh-and-blood or am I still an imprisoned, helpless, plotted being? Have you rescued me to reveal a plot of insane violence of which I am an unconscious part? If I burn and do not burn, it makes a difference . . .' He spoke with anger and the strangest humour. I felt a deep discomfiture in my dazed mind. This was an unusual and an absurd way of bringing home to me prisoners in gaols all over the world of whom I despaired for one reason or another. They were loathsome extensions of myself. No, I dismissed this as totally absurd. Extensions of myself – impossible! As such I would leave them there for ever like a figurine in a notebook or like a work of art that had no bearing on the future.

The Child-like man had been sentenced for stealing a boat akin to Queequeg's coffin that had rescued Ishmael in Herman Melville's *Moby Dick*. In addition I associated him with a gross and violent tale of rioters assaulting a prison in Harbourtown. From all this had seeped a sensation I could not control of desolation and uncertainty of the ranges of the land in the sea, the sea in the land. I had therefore shut him out of my arts – unconsciously perhaps – and consigned him again to my notebooks. He was buried history not living fiction . . .

I would leave him there in a prison or in a grave for ever. (I uneasily felt my quantum variations may have plucked him out but my mind was still dazed as to what I had done or was still doing . . .) Was he mad, I wondered, to remind me of Oceanic voyages I secretly wished to make, or to probe, or to understand more deeply than I had ever done before, Oceanic disappearances – within lost lands under the Seas – that I planned to execute as Quetzalcoatl had done, Oceanic returns of ancient Arthurian/Quetzalcoatlan gods that caught my attention in Montezuma's expectations of incorrigible, divine rights moving back from under or across the Seas?

Montezuma had doomed himself in such expectations. Would I doom myself like a well-cut sculpture with a growling, sophisticated, unnatural voice I brought from abroad into my studio?

Perhaps such returns of King Arthur of Camelot or of Quetzalcoatl would take apparently stable, regulated forms of submarines and torpedoes that concealed their blast until the last moment when the masters of the globe (as we saw them) blew the enemy to bits.

I thought of Sir Francis Drake. Was he a man of iron or of steel? It seemed incongruous and absurd that I should place a man honoured into divinity by a Queen – though a pirate and a robber – in league with modern submarines and torpedoes and with the Child-like prisoner. He (Drake) had not been buried and forgotten in a notebook of history. Most incongruous of all that I should place him with rioters assaulting a prison in an obscure town and port called Harbourtown.

And yet I saw with a curious sculptured mind – that cannot erase the slice of fame from infamy – a cut or connection between fiery men of steel and disabled prisoners whose flesh was ancient wood – so ancient they were sold as slaves and now were locked in cells – *I saw it with a dazed mind* and wondered at the void in cross-culturality.

Was there an inner, unperceived network between divinity (in its incorrigible shape) and robbery (in its self-appointed mastery of the globe), loathsomeness (concealed by flesh), love (that no one really knew save in paintings of beautiful families beyond which all others were the aliens)?

Turn this around as you wish. Call Drake the prisoner and the Child-like man the preferred art of a Queen. It still makes for a network and its extremities beyond absolutes which we have not perceived perhaps in the conscious arts of the world.

Fire dwelt in a hidden form in my map of the world that had been carven on the Stone that crashed into my studio. Fire is all-consuming. So it is written in the conventions that take materialism for their absolute. Fire blazes. *Yet fire has a quality that does not burn.* Non-burning qualities of fire are heresies. If fire has a quality that does not burn, though it seems all-consuming in material expression, then fire has partial forms in the arts of cross-culturality. We need to prove this in the roots of consciousness. Fire burns yet possesses a secret window, in the furnace of violence it creates, through which we contemplate an immense task in varieties of healing.

'Steel' embodies a metaphor of passion or of cold fire. The 'cold' is partial. 'Wood' embodies a metaphor of sculptured feeling or of passion *with* fire, though hidden in the stars (the suns) that blaze upon it. All 'feeling' in flesh or wood or steel or paint is a partiality drawn from range and depth. *The Promethean sufferings of Mankind are rooted in such enigmas.*

Am I not carven like sculptured wood or flesh in my studio? This is a disguise I wear which I cannot describe except in words of fiction, which bring Harbourtown into an edge of Space where Spirit varies passion and integrity. Does this not bring me into an unexpected relationship with a figurine I had planted in the prison of my notebooks? *The figurine grows.* It assumes forms I had not suspected in previous Dantesque and Platonic ages. It is not fixed.

Is it (or he) – I wondered with a dazed mind – the fiery/ non-fiery man of the art of a new civilization? A glimpse perhaps, no more than a glimpse. He is bottled up, it seems, in unconscious ways with which I have long struggled, in my studio, as an *inner* sculptured artist with *private* sculptures and paintings that turn to *public* flesh-and-blood. The quantum variations of such changes are many. Such inner sculptures within oneself and others are the beginnings of a subtle but enormous capacity for unpredictable freedoms and warnings and tragedies . . . It is a long way to go . . . Freedom cannot be taken for granted . . .

He hovers and wants to know whether I can rescue him, whether I can paint him, sculpt him, give him a spatial, dual reality that I have long sought for all my life.

He wears a beautiful suit – more expensive than any I could carve – which was cut, or woven, or fired in a great metropolis, London or Paris or Rome or New York, that closes around him still and conceals from him its conquistadorial derivations.

It gives him money to buy suits and cars and Stones, which

he claims were made by me, but steals his soul in the manufacture of imitations of genius, takes his veins, imitates them with leaden vessels, reduces them to wholly genetic functions, and pours into them the bloodstream of machines that is a likeness to itself...

He was a real man standing in my studio. I must say it but I feel an unreality about him in that I have begun to engage with the roots of consciousness. Perhaps this was true as well of the *exact* personification of the small sculpture of the Mother of Space in the woman in the Street. Not as exact as it appears. She had *grown* into a woman. But now all this had passed beyond an intuition. Curiously enough he (the man in my studio) was an obviously *inexact* personification of something I had been wrestling with for ages it seemed. Yet such inexactitudues brought home to me the life of pressures building in the unconscious through the arts one makes. I had accused him of being a spy who had crept, unknown to me, into my studio. He had broken into my book of notes. But now I wondered whether I might have imposed this on him. Was it not that with his coming – his throwing of the Stone that smashed into my studio – he had subconsciously arisen from the prison of my historical notebooks? Such prisons, such notebooks, were held in archives all over the world. I had begun to glimpse his background, as a figurine or a miniature, that I kept there, half-hidden, out of guilt, in my notebooks. The Mother of Space had grown to life from a small sculpture on the map of art in my studio. He had grown from a miniature I virtually hid in my notebooks. All such quantum variations – unreal or real as they seemed – were native to the roots of consciousness that take one totally by surprise and make one see that *life* is suddenly more mysterious than *fiction*. I could not believe it. I was a fiction-artist... Life has no fixed plot but brings gaps or gulfs into affairs that no one can account for save in speculative astronomy or philosophy. Within such gaps creeps the unconscious to alarm us with its unseen growth into a consciousness that remains unfinished, parts missing, parts of a story-line we would like to make. Story-lines are finished plots that we assume life to be but the roots of consciousness leave us uncertain of all such ends and beginnings and linear certainties ...

I remember now – with the vagueness of wood and of flesh – that he had accused me of being a rioter who had thrown the very Stone, which I held now in my hand, into a wall of the prison in Harbourtown. This had given him a chance to escape. *I had no memory of throwing the Stone.* He was jesting with an angry face that looked like living steel. Or was I seeking to open buried history in my notebooks to an art that grew from what seemed insubstantial roots into various edges of Space that needed to be tested and seen in the depths of recollection or they would prove a blind and tragic and perverse cross-culturality?

Was I involved in a vacancy of memory I could not wholly mask and it left a gap between my historical notebook and a fictional-seeming but real prison in Harbourtown?

Out of such vacancies the rioters now came like prisoners themselves guarding themselves with Cyclopean menaces of which they were unaware. I could not stop them. *I could not stop them.* They broke through my guilt into the unfinished arts that I pursued in a sensation of the roots of consciousness. I was dreaming ...

I recalled Quetzalcoatl and sought consolation from him in his absence or the insubstantial, various presence I had seen in the lines and triangles in the reclining woman.

Quetzalcoatl was dumbfounded, when he was reborn from the reclining woman – as he had been dumbfounded in the distant past – to find, on looking into a mirror, that his spirit could be clothed in an absolute, human Face, one pigment, one dominating appearance. This belied the variations of his presence.

All absolute Faces were corruptions that grew into racial and blinding stereotypes and concealed their cross-culturality. In their fixed, historical roles they could not see *through* their corruptions. They bombed populations into accepting them as incorrigible agents of a literal, man-sized divinity that became a diabolism leading them astray.

They left irreconcilable gaps they had shorn of a new learning, a new seeing, a new feeling. And wars were fought, political elections were consumed by rage, riots and assaults were conducted between blind history and blind history.

Stalin met Churchill and Roosevelt and parleyed with a cunning that made him the father of his people. They divided the world amongst themselves. As an ancient Pope had divided the world in the times of the Conquest of the pre-Columbian Americas. History seemed an absolute and a linear religion that led into fascism, beneath the temper of democracies, in absolute conglomerations forced into play by the mechanical strength of one on others, that Quetzalcoatl had dreaded.

I found myself looking closely at the man in my studio. His skin was like polished, dark, lighted steel or peculiar wood. His rich suit was beautifully tailored. And yet it seemed, in the blazing light of the room, to become a rag that he wore unconsciously on his wooden back. It fluttered a little, it shone like glass almost in the bright sunlight that brings into mottled play the grains on the glass that are hidden in a less shining moment when the present glare is absent.

Presence and absence are veined into cross-lighted materials like a pool that hardens and softens into blood, the blood of an inner sculpture.

This gave me a sensation of tragic cross-culturality.

A rich man had invoked the poor through rags of the future. His suit was destined to turn into rags.

I thought of revolutionary states that became fascist, or were already unconsciously fascist, in the present and the future. The flight of Time brought every absolute into the ragged scarecrow that it was or into the tyrannical status no one had perceived in depth or range.

History recorded events with an outer eye. It was a death that history foresaw. Flesh was divorced from the art of wood or glass or other substances (as unconscious/conscious growing or declining elements), from the art of blood as paint on the torpor of the still-ruling icon of a dismantling but menacing Self. Flesh-and-blood could become, in the anatomy of arts, the inner sculpture of sensitive, far-flung being which – by small degrees and shifts of crucial awareness – could enhance a measureless vocation rather than a tragic and a closed entertainment designed for a corrupt fixture and an incorrigible individualism.

I looked at the man in my studio and was smitten by fear. He had one hand in a pocket of his beautiful suit and I saw it was bunched over what appeared to be a gun. He had flung the Stone and now he was preparing to fire at me. I remembered that the carving I had made of him was unfinished. He was now inexact flesh-and-blood and seemed an unfinished, living copy of what I had uneasily made. His right hand had stirred the fear in me. It was assumed, I knew, that the right hand was an emblem of consciousness. This was a rash view of things. The right hand proved as unconscious of what it was doing, or had done, as the left was. I saw with fascination how the living surfaces of both hands were roughened and how a fist had disappeared into the cloth of his suit.

'Are you going to fire at me?' I demanded. My voice was hoarse, I thought. Did I speak from within myself, from the inner sculpture I carried within?

He looked so astonished that I was relieved. 'You seem to have a gun in your pocket.' The hoarseness persisted in the voice with which I spoke. I looked at him and weighed my chances. We possessed, it seemed, a glimmering non-burning quality that gave me hope.

The inexactitudes in his appearance stunned me now. I felt I could see through the cloth of his suit to the flesh of his arms and detect their roughened state. I could not actually do so but the impression persisted. I felt unnaturally guilty. I felt he belonged to my historical notebooks where unnatural, buried guilt presided in bunched guns in suits. But he was out in the rioting, upside-down arts I was making. Had I made him, had I sculpted him? Did this give me an inner feeling, shall I say, of the roughness of his skin and of the wealth that he possessed? Was he a living, scarred token of forests that had been ploughed into the ground?

He was laughing now with a trace of anger. 'Why do you think I would fire at you? I threw the Stone, I know, but it is yours. You invented it. You put the map of the world on it. The map is also here in this studio.' He was looking at the Mother of Space that stood on the map in my room.

'I am aware of myself as an artist and a god and a teacher...' I spoke apologetically.

'But why? Why should I kill you? Why do you fear? Is fear a new beginning that you do not understand? Is fear like inner wood, inner blocks that you need to sculpt to see they are as alive as I?' He was laughing wryly as if it were a deadly serious game we played in my studio.

'If you kill me' – I spoke in some desperation – 'and then kill yourself, no one would know why you acted as you did. No one would know . . .'

'Know what?'

'Know that I had failed to make you.' I was as desperate as ever. 'Not that I failed entirely. But cracks and gaps remained that I could not bridge.' I felt I had inadvertently and intuitively stumbled into new characterizations of fiction. Here was a real man in my studio. But he was an inexact, living copy of sculptures I had attempted within myself, without myself. Withinness and withoutness were wedded together in him and in me. I did not trust his voice. All voices are untrustworthy save in their bearing on an inner sculpture in the Stone of Time one carries in oneself. Was I attempting to *flesh* him, the *flesh* one makes inadvertently in the arts of the world? Was I fearful now of those arts and of what they could say in themselves?

'*You* made me?' He spoke with a quiet, laughing rage. Perhaps he despised me.

'Yes, I did.' I was still apologetic and fearful. 'You are a living copy – and it leaves me stunned – of what I made and am making of the world in which I live. How can I help but be involved again? It's a terrifying new beginning – as you say – that I have been approaching in my arts.'

'*Then* I am making you now. Making you *feel* the depths . . .' He stopped. His voice seemed to come from everywhere in my studio. His laughter echoed in the depths of every piece of sculpture and painting I had made. 'Yes, the depths,' he continued. 'Art springs from life. Or is it life that springs from art? You should know but you do not. Or are they both so related – in ways we have forgotten – that we fail to measure our unconscious motivations in our actions? As a consequence we make each other and we destroy each other mindlessly.' I felt his eyes boring into me like the knife with which I had cut them and sliced them into his head.

Then it was that my fear began to change. It did not melt away, it suffered a curious Sea-change, a Dream-change. I was dreaming though wide awake with a real man in my studio. *I looked through the beautiful cloth of his suit and saw what seemed a rag-and-bones body sliced into eyes. Those eyes looked at me as I looked into them. A curious Sea-creature he was.* Was this the flesh I was making? I was staggered. I was alarmed. I saw a man of the Sea, imprisoned for stealing a boat, who had been a lover of many women. Prisoner yet free in my Dream. Each woman that he had was secured by him through a divine rape. He felt himself to be a divine rapist even before he arrived fully on Earth. This gave him a dream of overwhelming mastery. My Dream laid bare his illusion of incorrigible control and Conquest. He was a man in my studio, normal as other men are, but prone to dreams of divinity. The Dream persisted in every affair he had. Until one day a woman, with whom he was engaged in sex, threw a Stone at his head. It fell into the Sea and broke him into two. He was fractured, he was broken, into the rag-and-bones I was now making. I felt dizzy, dumbfounded, alarmed. *He was broken.* Had he been broken by me? Was this the unconscious cause of my fear of him that gripped me and made me see a gun? *And then he knew a sensation of unspeakable tenderness, of compassion, he had never known all his life.* Non-burning fire blazed. It blazed and it almost died away like a star far out in Space. But a strong vestige of the undying, non-burning flame remained. And he raged at his ignorance. Did he not project his ignorance on me? It sprang from the relic he still experienced – that well-nigh blew him to bits – of an infinite compassion for all things. Was it a relic? Was it the blow of the Stone? Had it happened at the moment of his dismemberment? Had it happened afterwards when he was whole again? He felt whole despite his rag-and-bones flesh that I had put on him in the long apparently violent arts I performed with broken trees I had sliced into a universe of eyes.

We were caught in the terror of a world we touched for the first time, it seemed, in its divisions that we had taken for granted. Those divisions became whole unexpectedly but left us fearful of what we thought we had seen or felt. Such is the unconscious/conscious eruption of a Dream of a dream in art when a real man stands before us stripped, rich, poor, whole, broken.

He was as terrified as I was though we sought to conceal it from one another. Perhaps when he threw the Stone – as a relic of his love affair – and I accused him of carrying a gun we were inadvertently making an effort to bring into the open the dangerous, ignorant game men play with each other that gains a glimmer of non-burning fire when one is dismembered and the other sees through rich cloth to miraculous wood turning to bone and flesh and blood. They came in minute formations on relics of Space and may return to minuteness again. He felt himself afloat on the Stone that had been thrown at him and he had thrown at me. Such was my Dream as I looked at him. It was a Stone I had made and forgotten until this moment when a re-visionary process began in all my arts. I felt stripped too in confronting a real man as if he were a work of art. I felt embarrassed, humiliated, in straying so far from the paths of normal recognition and seeing him as he was, may have been, still could be. Was this a heresy I had been cultivating intuitively?

I shook myself out of my Dream. Not entirely but sufficiently to study the man who was before me in my studio. Had I rescued him and forgotten I had done so? Or was I still to rescue him from the prison of his suit in a body of rioters swarming everywhere from my notebooks? He was real. As real as Dream and reality. I had called him a spy but I was the greater spy in puncturing the rich cloth that he wore. New beginnings are as confusing as ancient origins.

Was it not in ancient times that an artist and a god, as vulnerable as I, sensed that the Stone of Time within himself carried a living body or bodies within minute formations of Space in itself? That Stone of universal, minute formations of creation might appear as grown marble outside himself but it was unfathomably related to the inner sculpture on which the artist worked in the sculptures and paintings he created.

A creative and re-creative relationship was endlessly established in which he was sculpted by what he was sculpting. He was being made by the Spirit of the arts he consulted in making and remaking others.

Had I become immersed in the creation of voices in bodies, rich, poor, tall, short, I scarcely knew though they figured in sculptures I made? No wonder they were stolen by immaterial, Carnival dancers, negligible, virtually forgotten that returned in the furies of Angels suppressed but real. Reality and unreality were in the nature of true art. The voice of the Mother of Space had been stolen and this was desolating until I met the reclining woman.

Was all this – in the form of the man in my studio – a symptom of Faustian, immortal Time that steals and brings back what it steals in unpredictable ways? It was and it was not. It was a radical penetration of Faustian Time away from a singular, absolute Face into mutualities between the negligible and the apparently fixed or formal, between upwards and downwards, between glimpses of the Sky that stretches into infinity and glimpses of the Earth that baffles life and finity, between loathing and love, between what one creates that re-creates the depths one has missed.

I had extended Van Gogh's limits in his last paintings in presenting the Chinese Immigrants into Harbourtown, South America. I had partially adopted Oscar Wilde's *Dorian Gray* as a medium in the arts through which I lived imaginatively in the prison though in my studio. Now I felt Goethe's Faust in a radical change of lines that led me back to Quetzalcoatlan Spirit...

Did Faustian Quetzalcoatl (in seeking a fragile bridge between past and present) form like a hopeful symbol across Space then dislodge itself afresh into a warning? *Suddenly I knew an acute sensation of disaster in the studio. I threw the Stone without thinking. It struck him in the ribs and in the arm. It broke his hand. The gun he had pulled from the pocket of his suit at the moment of the blow shifted in aim slightly. The bullet missed me and lodged in a wall in my studio. I felt a burning shock nevertheless. It struck my self-portrait – with its many faces – on the wall.* There was a rush of feet like the wings of a bird unconscious of itself. Three Harbourtown police officers appeared on the steps of the studio (had they come from above or below?) came through the door and seized the man.

'We saw him fly into your house,' they declared, terse-lipped, official, 'and felt we would wait awhile. We thought you were in league with him. Prisoners have escaped the gaol recently and it was rumoured that *you* instigated the weird schemes that they used. We see now we were wrong. He intended to kill you. He deceived you – he's an actor, he's a liar.'

I was stunned. My intuitions had gone wide of their mark except in confirmation of the fears I had felt. Intuition and counter-intuition, born of quantum art, bring characters that one makes into a living, other-side focus, as if to protest for a violent independence that could kill the maker as well without a deeper and a profound understanding of relationships between creature and unfathomable creator one has severed. Are they severed? Are they not flashingly alive? I saw his ragged flesh and broken body. I could not believe I had made this body in the Dream-time of art. Had I punctured the inner sculpture I carried within? A formidable, inner sculpture modelled, it seemed, by atrocities across the ages. Not easy to penetrate from whatever angle one came, from theatre, or studio, or mountain top, or valley, from ancient Mexico, or colonial Harbourtown as a gateway into the Americas. They were unconscious still of the links they carried that the police officers had deemed to be lies in their strait-jacketed word.

'Where did he get the rich suit?' I managed to ask.

'He stole it from a guard in the prison. A one-eyed rich guard he called him. He's full of stories.'

Goethe's Faust, in his implicit wide-ranging genius, had failed. Faust had not truly understood Quetzalcoatlan Spirit. The bridge between Western and pre-Columbian art – which may have existed in the unconscious – seemed broken. I saw that now. Van Gogh's late paintings, which extended themselves beyond their formal place and translated birds into ships on a cloudy Ocean of Space, had fused into blocks between Sky and Earth. He had shot himself. Perhaps he had been burdened by a knowledge he found impossible to plumb at the time.

Wilde's Dorian Gray had failed. It had been a notable attempt to bridge subjective place with the mysterious life of the arts that springs from a Stone of Time, but he was unable to make a further effort in that direction. He had been imprisoned and this had ruined him.

Such is the history of the arts that rule the world.

I had worked with mutualities in well-nigh forgotten, pre-Columbian arts and had sought additional gleanings from the greatest painters and writers in the West. Such gleanings were notable failures to transfigure an absolute Face as the ruling condition in global economy and politics. I had worked all my life to penetrate such a bland illusion. I had worked in creative and re-creative variations with wood and glass and paint to imply the unconscious in flesh-and-blood and this had brought me into an Imagination of making live flesh-and-blood sprung from sculptures and paintings I made in my studio that bore resemblances to the Stone of Time.

I had been deceived but had seen that counter-intuition is a quantum variation which brings characters into unpredictable and independent action, though I may have appeared to make them and to control them absolutely.

'One moment,' I said as they prepared to take him away, 'let me see him again. Do you think he intended to kill me? I swear I had an inkling but he denied this and seemed astonished I should think so.' Was this the theatre of the unconscious that deceives actor and audience about the nature of truth on which they fasten with one-sided words? Had he acted independently or had he been driven by unspoken fears arising in cultures the West had eclipsed?

The latter half of my utterance I spoke silently to myself. I looked into his eyes. They seemed to look at me from far away. Were they the eyes of the Child-like man of ancient pre-Columbian art I had kept hidden away in a notebook? Not entirely. I had propelled him onto an Ocean of Space like one coming from neglected areas of the Imagination upon a watershed of Times. But now this seemed a random play in the light of events that brought him five feet tall with a gun that he had fired at me. *Our fears, our long separations, had become a certainty in his eyes.* This was an instance of failures to move from linear fixations and philosophies and traditions. However grand these seemed they were inadequate in a dangerous world. They made little genuine provision for alterations of line or for apparently negligible variations that could breach conquistadorial habits secreted into institutional racism. I looked for the last time at the man they were holding. He was a real man. I had made a real man, if nothing else, from a dot in my notebooks. His was a reality that grew foot by foot. He was festered with a rich suit he had stolen from a one-eyed guard in the prison of his age. His neurosis mirrored mine in upside-down relationships, in the rich Cyclops of the modern world who had gained an economic innocence that filled me with despair.

I was tormented by a sensation of prisoners I had been asked to rescue but could not. They had no voice but the voice imposed by their gaolers. I sought to make flesh-and-blood, which was filled I now knew with fear, but the Cyclops were intent on human machines devoid of *Nobody* or of *Faceless*. Their iron teeth would consume them more easily.

Was it possible that a faint vestige of non-burning quality persisted between the man who had fired the gun and me?

Was there a longing and distant echo of an infinite compassion in the Stone I had flung at him, in the bullet he had fired at me like an actor in a remote, unscripted play? The News I heard every day was an unscripted play – without quantum variations – that offered no feeling or compassion for multiple deaths by gunfire or technological disasters. They were bundled into the mechanics at the centres of civilization. Yet I listened as closely as I could for a breath of incredible wholeness from implicitly broken body to implicitly broken body I had been making in upside-down rag-and-bones flesh from unconscious wood or glass or stone. Did each break signify an unscripted, creative gateway into an infinity of compassion, an infinity of love? I could not believe it but the listening feeling persisted into a non-burning quality that would require future Imaginations beyond me, future Imaginations that would link many-framed forms of music into the rhythms of language.

'This is Harbourtown,' I thought, 'an imaginary yet real town in South America. It follows the march of the masters of the globe. Can these masters deeply change and affect those who come after? Can those who come after affect the absolutes in the kings of wealth that are raised around us? Can art strike a different, mutual, cross-cultural path between consciousness and unconsciousness?'

My thoughts would have made no sense to the police. For them it was enough that I had escaped the shot that had been fired. They took the prisoner into a van in the Street. I listened and heard the Clock strike. It struck with the Sun glinting on a painting I had made. The van moved away and was lost to sight. The intricate movement of the Sun, a painting of light, spoke of edges of Space and planetary conditions that were invisible though real. Art is real. We were real, however invisible to others in distant spaces I had sought to bring into play in unfathomable yet partially fathomable ways in human elements.